The Adventures of
PINOCCHIO

The Adventures of
PINOCCHIO
by Carlo Collodi

Translated and illustrated by
Francis Wainwright

HENRY HOLT AND COMPANY
NEW YORK

To
Sheila, my wife

First published in the United States in 1986 by
Henry Holt and Company, Inc., 521 Fifth Avenue,
New York, New York 10175.
Originally published in Great Britain.

Library of Congress Catalog Card Number: 86-45047

The color artwork was prepared by using Winsor and
Newton gouache on Canson bristol paper.
Typeset in 13 on 16 pt Trump Medieval
by Wyvery Typesetting Ltd., Bristol

ISBN:0-8050-0027-5

First American Edition

Designer: Zena Flax
Printed in Great Britain
10 9 8 7 6 5 4 3 2 1

ISBN 0-8050-0027-5

Contents

Translator's Note

This is my tribute to the author of the greatest of Italian children's classics.

It is the direct result of a first visit, in 1965, to Collodi, the Tuscan village, where it all started, so long ago.

Carlo Lorenzini took both his inspiration and pen-name from this his mother's birthplace. His great love for the village and the Tuscan hills shines through every word in the Pinocchio saga, and for more than 20 years, I too have lived under that same spell.

Pinocchio, Geppetto, Fire-Eater and the ever loving, long suffering Blue-Fairy, have all remained in my heart, and my dream of translating and illustrating a version as close as is possible to this 19th. century masterpiece, has finally come true.

A labour of love.

Long live Pinocchio!

FW

CHAPTER ONE

*Master Cherry, the Carpenter,
finds a piece of wood*

Oɴᴄᴇ ᴜᴘᴏɴ ᴀ ᴛɪᴍᴇ there was . . . No, not a King. Once upon a time there was a piece of wood. Just a perfectly ordinary log for a cosy, winter fire.

This particular piece of wood happened to be in the workshop of an old carpenter. His name was Master Antonio, but everyone called him Master Cherry because the end of his nose was always red and shiny, just like a ripe cherry.

As soon as Master Cherry set eyes on the log he beamed with delight. He rubbed his hands together with satisfaction, and said softly to himself, "This wood is just what I want to make a table leg."

He quickly picked up his sharp axe to strip the bark and cut it into shape. His hand was raised ready to strike the first blow when he hesitated, for he had heard a tiny voice which implored him: "Don't hit me too hard!"

Master Cherry glanced round the shop in a fright to see where that little voice could have come from, but he saw no one. He looked under his workbench. No one there! He looked inside a cupboard which he always kept locked; no one there. He looked in his basket of wood shavings and sawdust. No one there. He even opened the workshop door and looked up and down the street, but there was no one.

"I must have imagined it!" he said at last, laughing and scratching his wig. "Back to work."

He took up his axe again and down it came on the wood.

"Oh, you're hurting me!" cried that same little voice. This time Master Cherry was thunderstruck. His eyes almost popped out of his head with fright; his mouth was wide open, and his tongue lolled over his chin like a gargoyle.

As soon as he could speak he said, trembling and stammering: "But where did that little voice come from? There's not a living soul here. Has this piece of wood learned to cry and complain just like a child? I can't believe it. It's only firewood after all. Could someone be hidden inside it? If there is, so much the worse for him. I'll soon fix him!"

And so he began to beat the wood against the wall without mercy. Then he stopped and listened to see if any little voice complained this time. He waited two minutes – nothing; five minutes – nothing; ten minutes – and still nothing!

"No!" he exclaimed, forcing himself to laugh. "I must have imagined that little voice. Come on! Back to work."

And because he felt very afraid, he began to sing to give himself courage.

Meanwhile, he put his axe down and taking up his plane he began to smooth and shape the piece of wood. But while the plane went backwards and forwards, he heard that little voice. It was laughing: "Stop! You're tickling me!"

This time poor Master Cherry fell down as if struck by lightning. When he opened his eyes he was sitting on the floor. You wouldn't have recognised him. Fright had turned the tip of his nose from bright red to blue.

Aт THAT MOMENT there was a knock on the door. "Come in," said the carpenter, who did not even have the strength to get up.

A brisk, lively old man walked into the workshop. His name was Geppetto, but when the boys in the neighbourhood wanted to tease him they called him Corn-Cob, because he wore a bright yellow wig.

Geppetto was very quick-tempered and woe betide anyone who called him Corn-Cob!

"Good morning, Master Antonio," said Geppetto, "what are you doing down there on the floor?"

"I'm teaching the ants the alphabet, of course."

"Much good may it do you!"

"What brings you here, Master Geppetto?"

"My legs, of course. But Master Antonio, I have come to ask you a favour."

"Here I am, at your service," replied the carpenter, getting to his knees.

"I had an idea this morning."

"Let's hear it then."

"I thought I'd make a wooden puppet, a really fine one, that can dance, and fence, and turn cartwheels. Then, together, we could travel the world, and earn an honest crust of bread and a glass of wine or two. What do you think?"

"Good for you, Corn-Cob!" cried that mysterious little voice.

Master Geppetto became so angry that he turned bright red, just like a ripe tomato, and said in a rage: "Why do you insult me?"

"Who's insulting you?"

"You called me Corn-Cob!"

"I did not!"

"Yes you did!"

"No! I did not."

"Yes you did!"

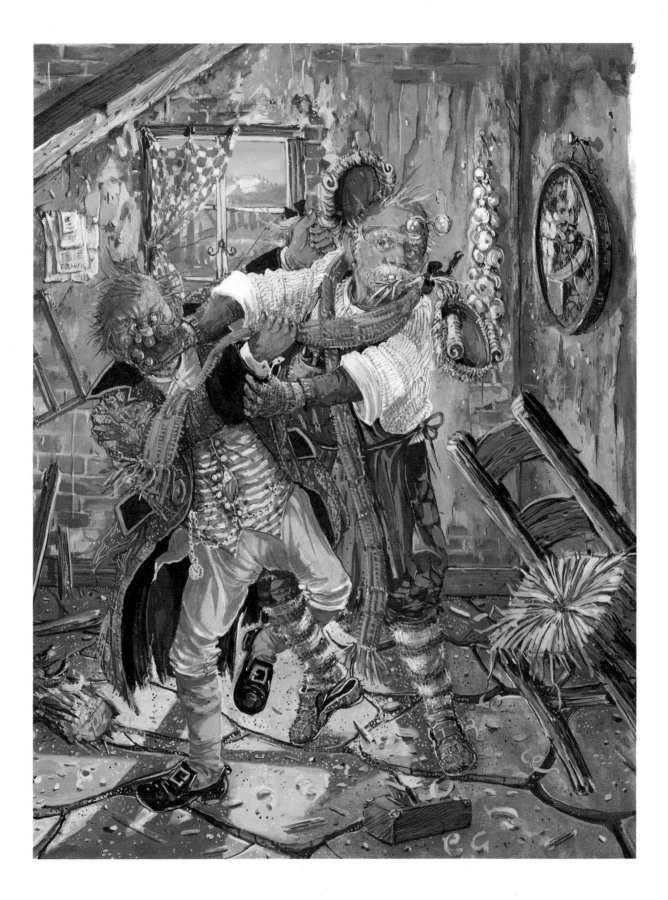

And getting more and more excited, they grabbed at one another's wigs, and slapped and bit and scratched each other.

At the end of the fight Master Antonio found Geppetto's yellow wig in his hands, and Geppetto had the carpenter's grey wig between his teeth.

"Give me back my wig," said Master Antonio.

"And you give me back mine, and let's make our peace."

So the two little old men put their wigs back on, shook hands, and vowed to be good friends as long as they lived.

"Now, Geppetto," said the carpenter, just to show that they were good friends again, "what can I do for you?"

"I would like a little piece of wood to make my puppet."

Master Antonio was delighted and quickly went to his bench and picked up the piece of wood that had frightened him so. But just as he was giving it to his friend, it wriggled so hard that it slipped out of his hands, and struck poor Geppetto hard on the shin.

"Ah! This is a fine way to make me a present, Master Antonio! You've almost lamed me."

"Upon my honour, I didn't do it!"

"Oh, so *I* did it then!"

"It's all the fault of this piece of wood . . ."

"Yes, I know it was the wood that struck me, but it was *you* who threw it at my leg!"

"I did not throw it at you!"

"Liar!"

"Now, Geppetto, don't insult me or I'll call you Corn-Cob!"

"Ass!"

"Corn-Cob!"

"Donkey!"

"Corn-Cob!"

"Ugly monkey!"

"Corn-Cob!"

When he heard himself called Corn-Cob for the third time, Geppetto, blind with rage, rushed at the carpenter, and the second battle was even worse than the first.

When it was all over, Master Antonio had two more scratches on his nose and Geppetto, two buttons less on his waistcoat. They agreed it was a draw, shook hands again, and vowed to be good friends as long as they lived.

Then Geppetto picked up his piece of wood, thanked Master Antonio, and limped home.

CHAPTER THREE

*Geppetto goes home and
makes his puppet*

GEPPETTO LIVED IN A little room on the ground floor. It was lit by a small window under the stairs. His furniture could not have been simpler. One rickety chair, a shaky bed, and a broken-down old table. At the back of the room a fireplace could be seen with a good fire in it; but the fire was only painted, and over the painted fire was a painted pot, which was boiling merrily and sending forth clouds of steam, just like real steam.

As soon as he was home, Geppetto took up his tools and began to carve his puppet.

"What shall I call him?" he said to himself. "I think I'll call him Pinocchio because that name will bring him good luck. I once knew a whole family of Pinocchios and they all got along splendidly. The richest one of them was a beggar."

When he had thought of a name for the puppet he set to work with a will. He quickly made his hair, and his forehead, and his eyes.

As soon as the eyes were finished, he was amazed to see them move, and stare at him intently.

When Geppetto saw those two wooden eyes watching him, he didn't like it at all, and he said crossly: "Naughty wooden eyes, why are you looking at me?" But no one answered.

Next he made the nose; but as soon as it was finished it began to grow. It grew and it grew until it seemed as if it would never stop.

Poor Geppetto worked as fast as he could to shorten it, but the more he shortened it, the longer the nose became.

After the nose he made the mouth; but before he had finished it, it began to laugh and poke fun at him. "Stop laughing!" said Geppetto irritably, but he might as well have spoken to the wind.

"Stop laughing!" he threatened.

The mouth stopped laughing and then stuck out its tongue. Geppetto did not want to spoil the puppet, so he pretended not to see it, and went on with his work.

After the mouth he made the chin, then the neck, the shoulders, the stomach, the arms, and the hands.

The moment the hands were finished, Geppetto's wig was snatched from his head. He looked up. There was his yellow wig in the puppet's hands.

"Pinocchio! Give me back my wig this minute!"

But Pinocchio, instead of returning the wig, put it on his own head, and was almost hidden under it.

This insolence made Geppetto sadder than he had ever felt in his whole life. He turned to Pinocchio and said: "You rascal! I haven't even finished you yet, and already you're disobeying your father! That's bad, my boy, very bad indeed!"

And he wiped away a tear.

When Geppetto had finished the feet, a kick landed on his nose.

"It serves me right," he said to himself. "I should have thought of that before! Now it's too late."

He picked up the puppet and placed him on the floor to see if he could walk; but Pinocchio's legs were too stiff, and he didn't know how to move them. So Geppetto took him by the hand and showed him how to put one foot in front of the other.

When the stiffness wore off Pinocchio began to walk by himself, and run round the room; and finally he slipped out of the door and off he ran down the street.

Poor Geppetto ran after him as fast as he could but he could not catch him, for the little rascal leaped like a hare, and his wooden feet clattered on the pavement, making as much noise as twenty pairs of clogs.

"Catch him! Catch him!" cried Geppetto; but when the people in the street saw Pinocchio running by as fast as a racehorse, they stared at him in amazement, then they began to laugh and laugh until their sides ached.

At last, by some lucky chance, a policeman appeared. When he heard the noise he really thought a horse had got away from its master; so very bravely he planted himself in the middle of the street with his legs wide apart, determined to stop it and prevent any further trouble.

Pinocchio from far off saw the policeman and decided to run straight through his legs; but the policeman, without moving, picked him up neatly by the nose and returned him to Geppetto, who wanted to pull his ears to punish him. But to his annoyance he couldn't find any ears to pull. He'd been in such a hurry, he had forgotten to make him any.

So he grabbed him by the scruff of the neck, and as they walked away he said, threateningly: "Come home, I'll settle with you there!"

At this ominous remark Pinocchio threw himself on the ground and refused to budge. A crowd of busybodies soon gathered round him: "That poor puppet!" some of them exclaimed. "He is right not to want to go home! Who knows how dreadfully old Geppetto might beat him!"

And others added maliciously: "Geppetto *seems* a good man, but he is a perfect tyrant with children. If we leave that poor puppet in his hands, why, he's capable of tearing him to pieces!"

So the policeman let Pinocchio go free, and decided instead to put Geppetto in prison. Geppetto could say nothing in his own defence as he was crying like a calf that's lost its mother, and as they marched towards the prison he sobbed: 'Wretched son! And to think I worked so hard to make him into a fine puppet! But I deserve it. I should have known what to expect!"

CHAPTER FOUR

*Pinocchio and the
Talking Cricket*

PINOCCHIO RAN HOME across the fields as quickly as possible. He was in such a hurry he jumped over high banks and thorn hedges, and ditches full of murky water, just like a little goat or a hare running away from the hunters.

When he got home, the door was ajar. He went in and locked it securely behind him. He then threw himself down on the floor with a sigh of relief.

But the relief didn't last long, for he heard something in the room saying: "Cree, Cree, Cree!"

"Who's calling me?" said Pinocchio, scared stiff.

"It is I."

Pinocchio turned and saw a large cricket crawling slowly up the wall.

"Who are you?"

"I'm the Talking Cricket and I have lived in this room for more than a hundred years."

"Well, this is my room now and you'll oblige me by leaving this instant."

"I shall not leave," replied the Talking Cricket, "until I have told you a few home truths."

"Well then be quick about it!"

"Woe to those children who disobey their parents, and who run away from home. They'll never be happy in this world, and sooner or later they'll regret it bitterly."

"Sing your heart out, Cricket, but tomorrow, at sunrise, I'm off because if I stay here I'll be sent to school, and by hook or by crook, I'll be made to do lessons, just like other children. Now I'll tell you a secret, I don't intend to study at all; I shall be far happier chasing butterflies, and climbing trees, and robbing birds' nests."

"You poor fool! Don't you realise that if you do that you'll grow up a donkey, and everyone will laugh at you?"

"Be quiet, you stupid Cricket!" cried Pinocchio.

But the Cricket, who was very patient and quite a philosopher, was not offended. He just went on talking.

"All right, if you don't want to go to school, why don't you learn a trade? Then, at least, you could earn a living."

"Let me tell you something," replied Pinocchio. "Out of all the trades in the world do you know which suit me best?"

"No," said the Cricket.

"Eating, drinking, sleeping, having fun and being lazy from morning till night."

"Let me tell *you* something," said the Talking Cricket, calm and patient as ever, "he who follows those trades almost always ends up in the hospital or the prison."

"Watch out, you horrid Cricket, don't put a jinx on me, or you'll make me angry and it'll be all the worse for you!"

"Poor Pinocchio! I do feel sorry for you!"

"Why are you sorry for me?"

"Because you're a puppet and what's worse, you're a puppet with a wooden head."

At these words Pinocchio lost his temper completely. He seized a mallet from the bench and hurled it at the Talking Cricket.

Perhaps he did not intend to hit him but unluckily the mallet struck the cricket right on the head. The poor creature only had time to say "Cree, Cree, Cree," before he was flattened on the wall.

CHAPTER FIVE

Pinocchio is hungry

IT BEGAN TO GROW DARK, and Pinocchio remembered that he had had nothing to eat all day. He was so ravenous by now that he could have eaten a horse.

Pinocchio ran to the fireplace where the pot was boiling and put his hand out to lift the lid to see what was cooking, but, of course, the pot was only painted on the wall.

What a disappointment! His nose, which was already too long, grew several inches longer.

He ran about the room and searched in every nook and cranny for a little bread, even stale bread. He would have been grateful for anything – a crust, or a bone left by a dog, mouldy old porridge, a fish bone, or even a cherry stone. But he found nothing, absolutely nothing.

Meanwhile, he grew hungrier every moment, but all he could do was yawn. He yawned such enormous yawns that his mouth reached right back to his ears, or where they should have been had he had any; and after he had finished yawning he tried spitting, but his stomach still felt empty.

At last, in despair, he began to weep: "That Talking Cricket was right, I was wrong to disobey my father and run away. If my father were here now, I shouldn't be yawning myself to death."

Suddenly, in a pile of rubbish, he saw something white, it looked like an egg! Pinocchio pounced on it. It was an egg! He was overjoyed but he feared he might be dreaming.

"Now, how shall I cook it?" Pinocchio hesitated and finally decided: "I'll poach it!"

No sooner said than done. He set a little pan on a brazier of lighted charcoal, put some water in it, instead of oil or butter. When the water began to boil, crack, he broke the eggshell and held it over the pan.

But instead of the yolk and white of an egg, a little chick flew out, and making a polite bow, said cheerfully: "A thousand thanks, Master Pinocchio, for having spared me the trouble of breaking my shell! Good-bye, take care, and give my love to everyone!"

With that the chick spread its wings, flew through the open window, and was gone.

When Pinocchio had recovered a little he began to cry, and scream, and stamp his feet in despair.

His stomach felt emptier than ever, and since he could find nothing to put in it he thought he would go into the village again. Some kind person might give him a little bread.

CHAPTER SIX

Pinocchio goes to sleep

IT WAS A BITTERLY COLD night. Thunder cracked and lightning flashed as though the heavens were on fire. A fierce wind whistled angrily, raising clouds of dust, and making all the trees bend and groan as if in torment.

Pinocchio was dreadfully afraid of thunder and lightning, but his hunger was greater than his fear, so he ran as fast as he could to the village. He arrived there with his tongue hanging out.

But all was dark and silent. The shops were closed, the doors of all the houses were locked tight, there wasn't even a stray dog to be seen. It seemed like a ghost town.

However, Pinocchio's hunger and despair made him give a long, long ring at the doorbell of one of the houses, saying to himself: "Someone is sure to answer!"

And, in fact, an energetic old man in a nightcap looked out of the window and shouted crossly: "What do you want? It's terribly late."

"Would you be so kind as to give me a little piece of bread?"

"Wait, I'll be right back!" replied the old man.

In half a minute the window was opened again, and the man called to Pinocchio: "Stand under the window, and hold out your cap!"

Pinocchio did as he was told and a great pan full of water rained down on him, drenching him from head to foot, just like a wilted plant.

He went home wet as a drowned rat, and almost dead with fatigue and hunger. He could not stand up any longer and so he sat down, and put his wet, muddy feet in the warm brazier.

In this position he soon fell fast asleep, and while he was sleeping, his wooden feet caught fire, and slowly burned to ashes.

Pinocchio slept and snored, feeling nothing. At last at daybreak, he was roused by someone knocking on the door.

"Who is it?" he called, yawning and rubbing his eyes.

"It's me!" replied a voice.

It was Geppetto.

CHAPTER SEVEN
Geppetto comes home

POOR PINOCCHIO'S EYES were still half-shut, and he had not noticed that his feet were burned away; so when he heard his father's voice he jumped down from his stool to run and draw the bolt. But after staggering a little way he fell flat on his face, with a noise like a whole bag of wooden spoons falling from a fifth storey window.

"Open the door!" cried Geppetto.

"I can't, Father," replied the puppet, bursting into tears and rolling over and over on the floor.

"Why not?"

"Because someone has eaten my feet!"

"And who could have done that?"

"The cat," said Pinocchio, as he caught sight of the cat playing with some wood shavings.

"Do as I ask, open the door!" cried Geppetto again. "How can the cat have harmed you?"

"Honestly, I can't stand up. Oh, poor me! poor me! I shall have to walk on my knees for the rest of my life!"

Geppetto thought that all this fuss was just another of the puppet's tricks so he climbed up the wall and went in through the window.

At first he was furious; but when he saw his own dear Pinocchio lying on the floor without any feet, his anger melted away.

He took him in his arms, kissed and patted him, and with tears streaming down his face, said through his sobs: "My dear little Pinocchio, how did your feet get burned away?"

"I don't know, Father, but it's been a dreadful night. I shall never forget it as long as I live." As he told Geppetto what had happened Pinocchio began to cry and scream so loudly that he could have been heard for miles around.

Geppetto only understood from the jumble of words that the puppet was dying of hunger. He took three pears out of his pocket, and said, as he gave them to him: "These three pears were for my breakfast; but I'll gladly give them to you. Eat them, and I hope they do you good."

"If you want me to eat them, you'll have to peel them for me."

"Peel them for you?" cried Geppetto in astonishment. "I'd never have believed that you could be so fussy. We should always eat whatever's set before us, and be grateful because you never know what may happen."

"That's all very well," replied Pinocchio, "but I shan't eat any fruit that hasn't been peeled first. I can't stand peel."

So the patient and kind Geppetto took out his pocket knife and peeled the three pears, putting all the peel carefully to one side on the table.

When Pinocchio had taken two bites out of the first pear, he was about to throw away the core, but Geppetto stopped him.

"Don't throw it away, it might come in useful."

"You don't think I'm going to eat the core, do you?" cried Pinocchio, turning to him angrily.

"Who knows! You may have to."

So the three cores were put with the peel.

When he had eaten, or rather, devoured the three pears, Pinocchio stretched himself, yawned, and then began to whine: "I'm still hungry!"

"But, my dear son, I have nothing more to give you."

"Nothing, nothing at all?"

"Only this peel and these cores."

"Oh all right!" said Pinocchio, "if there's really nothing else, I might as well eat a bit of this peel."

And he began to eat. At first he pulled a face, but soon all the peel was gone; and then he ate the cores, one by one. When he had finished everything, he patted his stomach and said cheerfully: "Now I feel better!"

"You see," said Geppetto, "why you shouldn't be so fussy."

CHAPTER EIGHT

*Geppetto makes Pinocchio
two new feet*

PINOCCHIO WAS NO LONGER hungry but then he began to whimper and grumble because he wanted two new feet.

But Geppetto let him cry and complain for half the day. At last he said: "Why should I make you new feet? So that you can run away again?"

"I promise," said the sobbing puppet, "that from now on I'll be as good as gold."

"That's what all children say when they want something," replied Geppetto.

"I promise to go to school every day, and work hard, and make you proud of me . . ."

"That's what all children say when they want something."

"But I'm not like other children! I'm better than any of the others, and I always tell the truth. I promise I will learn a trade and be a comfort to you in your old age."

Although Geppetto tried to look very fierce, his eyes filled with tears, and his heart was sad when he saw his poor Pinocchio in such a dreadful state. He did not say a word, but picked up his tools and two little pieces of well-seasoned wood and began to work as fast as he could.

In less than half an hour the feet were finished; and they were two of the most stylish, swiftest feet ever carved, as fine a pair as any sculptor could have made.

Then Geppetto said: "Shut your eyes, I've got a surprise for you."

Pinocchio shut his eyes and pretended to fall asleep; meanwhile Geppetto melted some glue in an eggshell, and carefully stuck the feet in place. He did it so neatly that you couldn't see where they joined the legs.

As soon as the puppet felt his new feet, he jumped down from the table and began to jump and dance around the room, he was so happy.

"Now, to show you how grateful I am," said Pinocchio to his father, "I want to go to school this very minute."

"What a good boy you are!"

"But I need some clothes."

Geppetto was a poor man; in fact, he hadn't a penny in the world: so all he could do was re-paint Pinocchio from head to toe. Pinocchio ran to look at his reflection in a basin full of water, and he was so pleased with what he saw that he strutted round the room shouting: "I look just like a prince!"

"Yes, indeed," replied Geppetto, "but remember, it is not only fine clothes that make a prince but clean clothes too."

"There's still something missing and it's the most important thing of all," said Pinocchio.

"What's that?"

"I haven't got a Spelling Book."

"You're right; but how shall we get one?"

"That's easy! Go to the bookshop and buy one."

"And where shall I get the money?"

"Well, I haven't any," said the puppet.

"Neither have I," added the old man sadly.

Pinocchio understood what that meant and he grew sad too.

"Never mind!" cried Geppetto suddenly, and jumped up and put on his tattered old overcoat and ran out of the house.

He was soon back with a Spelling Book; but the poor man was in his shirt-sleeves, and it was freezing cold outside, and snowing.

"Where's your overcoat, Father?"

"I've sold it."

"Why did you do that?"

"It made me too warm."

Pinocchio understood at once and he was so overcome that he threw his arms around Geppetto's neck and kissed him all over his face.

CHAPTER NINE

Pinocchio sells his new
Spelling Book

WHEN IT STOPPED snowing, Pinocchio took his fine new Spelling Book and set off for school. On the way he made all sorts of plans and built thousands of castles in the air, each one more beautiful than the other.

"Today I'll learn to read; tomorrow I'll learn to write, and the day after tomorrow I'll learn arithmetic. Then I'll be so well educated that I can earn piles of money; and with the very first pennies I earn I'll buy my father the warmest overcoat made from the finest cloth. No, not cloth, it shall be all gold and silver, with diamond buttons. He deserves nothing but the best."

Suddenly he heard the distant sounds of a fife and drum: fi-fi-fi-fi . . . rat-a-tat-tat.

He stopped and listened. The music came from the end of a long street that crossed the one which led to the school. At the end of that long street lay a small village and the sea.

"What's that music? What a shame that I've got to go to school!"

He hesitated and then made up his mind: "Today I'll listen to music, and tomorrow I'll go to school. There's always plenty of time for school."

And off he ran. The further he ran the more distinctly he heard the fifes and drum: fi-fi-fi-fi, fi-fi-fi, rat-a-tat-tat . . . fi-fi-fi.

He soon found himself in a little square full of people all crowding round a large brightly painted booth made of wooden boards and canvas.

"What's that big building?" inquired Pinocchio, turning to one of the local boys.

"Read the posters."

"I don't know how to read today."

"Dunce! Then I'll read it for you:

FIRE-EATER'S STUPENDOUS MARIONETTE THEATRE

"Has the play started yet?"

"It's just about to."

"How much is it to go in?"

"Four pence."

Pinocchio was so excited that quite unashamedly he asked the boy: "Lend me four pence till tomorrow."

"I'd love to," said the boy laughing at him, "but I can't today."

"You can have my jacket for four pence," said the puppet.

"What do I want with your jacket? It's only painted on anyway."

"Will you buy my shoes?"

"They're only good for firewood."

Pinocchio hesitated, and stammered, and at last he said it: "Will you give me four pence for this brand new Spelling Book?"

"I'm only a little boy and I don't buy things from other little boys," said the child.

"I'll give you four pence for the Spelling Book," cried a rag and bone man, who had overheard the conversation. So in a few seconds, the book was sold while Geppetto slaved away, shivering in his shirt sleeves.

CHAPTER TEN

The marionettes recognise
Pinocchio as one of them

WHEN PINOCCHIO ENTERED the theatre he nearly caused a riot.

The curtain was up and the play had already begun.

Harlequin and Punchinello were on stage and quarrelling as usual, threatening to come to blows at any moment.

The audience were enthralled. But all at once Harlequin stopped acting and, turning towards the audience, he pointed to the back of the theatre, and shouted, in his best stage manner: "Heavens above! Am I awake, or am I dreaming? That must be Pinocchio over there!"

"Yes, it is Pinocchio!" cried Punchinello.

"It's Pinocchio! It's Pinocchio!" shouted all the marionettes in chorus, running out of the wings. "It's Pinocchio! Here's our little brother

Pinocchio! Hurray for Pinocchio!"

"Come up on to the stage, Pinocchio," cried Harlequin.

So Pinocchio jumped from the back of the theatre to the front seats; and, with another jump, he landed on the conductor's head, and from there made a flying leap on to the stage into the arms of the marionettes, who overwhelmed him with loving hugs and kisses.

When the audience saw that the play had stopped they began to shout: "The play! The play! Get on with the play!"

They were wasting their breath. The marionettes only redoubled their cries of joy and, putting Pinocchio on their shoulders, they carried him in triumph down to the footlights.

Suddenly, Fire-Eater, the showman, appeared. He was very tall and so ugly that it frightened you just to look at him. His beard was like a smear of jet black ink and it was so long that it came right down to the ground, and he stepped on it when he walked. His mouth was as large as an oven; his eyes were like two red lanterns, and he was cracking a great whip, made of serpents' and foxes' tails, all twisted together.

When Fire-Eater appeared no one dared breathe and the marionettes trembled like leaves on a tree.

"Why have you come here to ruin my show?" he asked Pinocchio, in a voice that thundered like a giant with a bad cold.

"Please, your Honour, it wasn't my fault."

"Not another word! I'll settle with you later."

As soon as the play was over, Fire-Eater went into the kitchen. He was roasting a whole sheep for his supper, and it was turning slowly on the spit over the fire. When he saw that there was not enough wood to finish cooking it, he called for Harlequin and Punchinello and said to them: "Bring me that puppet I hung up on a nail. He's made of nice dry wood."

At first Harlequin and Punchinello hesitated; but Fire-Eater glared at them so menacingly that they obeyed.

They returned to the kitchen carrying Pinocchio, who was squirming like an eel out of water, and shrieking desperately: "Oh Father, save me! I don't want to die!"

CHAPTER ELEVEN
Fire-Eater sneezes

FIRE-EATER LOOKED HORRIBLE. But at heart he wasn't really so bad. He began to feel sorry for Pinocchio. Although he tried to stop himself, he couldn't help it . . . he sneezed with all his might.

Harlequin had been looking as sorrowful as a weeping willow, but when he heard that great sneeze his face brightened and he whispered to Pinocchio: "Good news, little brother. When Fire-Eater sneezes, that's a sure sign he feels sorry for you. You're saved!"

After Fire-Eater had sneezed, he continued to speak gruffly and shouted at Pinocchio: "Stop that blubbering! It gives me stomach ache . . . it aches so much that . . . that . . . a-tchoo! a-tchoo!" – and this time he sneezed twice in a row.

"God Bless you!" said Pinocchio, politely.

"Thank you. And are your mother and father still alive?" asked Fire-Eater.

"My father is but I never knew my mother."

"How sorry your old father would be if I threw you on the fire! Poor old man. How I pity him! A-tchoo! a-tchoo! a-tchoo!" – and he sneezed three times.

"God Bless you!" cried Pinocchio again.

"Thank you. On the other hand you should really feel sorry for me because, as you see, I haven't enough wood to finish roasting my supper. You'd just have done it. Never mind, I'll put one of my other marionettes on the fire instead. Ho there, police!"

Two wooden policemen appeared immediately.

Fire-Eater said in a hoarse voice: "Take Harlequin, tie him up and throw him on the fire. My mutton must be well done!"

Harlequin was so terrified that his legs gave way under him, and he fell flat on his face.

Pinocchio was so upset he threw himself at Fire-Eater's feet and wept such a flood of tears that he drenched the whole of the great black beard. He

cried imploringly: "Have mercy, Master!"

"There are no masters here!" replied Fire-Eater sternly.

"Have mercy, Your Excellency!"

Fire-Eater pursed his lips, and, suddenly melting a little, he said to Pinocchio: "Well, what can I do for you?"

"I beg you, please spare poor Harlequin!"

"Don't ask me that. If I spare you, I must put him on the fire to cook my supper."

"In that case," cried Pinocchio, rising to his feet, "I know my duty. Forward, policemen! Tie me up, and throw me on the fire."

Everyone began to weep.

At first Fire-Eater remained as hard and cold as a block of ice; but then, little by little, he began to melt, and to sneeze. When he had sneezed four or five times, he opened his arms affectionately to Pinocchio, saying: "You're a wonderful boy! Come here and give me a kiss."

Pinocchio climbed up Fire-Eater's beard like a squirrel, and gave him a resounding kiss right on the top of his nose.

"And am I spared?" asked Harlequin, in a trembling voice.

"You're spared," replied Fire-Eater; then he added, as he shook his head: "Never mind! Tonight I suppose I'll have to eat my supper half-cooked, but another time it will be somebody's turn, mark my words!"

When they knew that their brothers were safe, all the marionettes ran on to the stage, lit all the lights, as if it were a gala performance, and skipped and danced until the sun rose next morning.

CHAPTER TWELVE

Fire-Eater gives Pinocchio
five gold pieces to
take to his father

THE NEXT DAY FIRE-EATER called Pinocchio to one side and asked him: "What is your father's name?"

"Geppetto."

"And what does he do?"

"He's a poor man."

"I see. And does he earn very much doing that?"

"He earns just so much that he has never a penny in his pocket. He even had to sell his overcoat to buy me a Spelling Book so that I could go to school: it was only an old tattered overcoat, too!"

"Poor fellow! I almost feel sorry for him. Here are five gold pieces. Go quickly and give them to him, with my compliments."

Pinocchio thanked Fire-Eater a thousand times. He gave everyone a big hug then, very happy, he set off for home.

But before he had travelled very far he met a Fox, who was lame in one paw, and a Cat, who was blind in both eyes. They were hobbling along as best they could, like good friends in adversity. The lame Fox was leaning on the Cat, and the blind Cat was being guided by the Fox.

"Good morning, Pinocchio," said the Fox politely.

"How do you know my name?" asked the puppet.

"I know your father very well."

"Where did you see him?"

"Yesterday in the doorway of his house."

"And what was he doing?"

"He was in his shirtsleeves, and shivering with cold."

"Poor Father! Thank Heavens he won't have to suffer the cold any longer."

"Why not?"

"Because I'm a rich man."

"You? A rich man?" said the Fox and he began to laugh scornfully. The Cat laughed, too, but he stroked his whiskers with his paw to conceal the fact.

"It's not funny," cried Pinocchio irritably. "These, for your information, are five gold pieces."

And from his pocket he took the money Fire-Eater had given him.

The sound of jingling coins worked a miracle. Fox moved his lame leg and Cat opened wide his blind eyes; but he shut them again so quickly that Pinocchio never even noticed.

"And now," inquired the Fox, "what are you going to do with this money?"

"First of all," answered the puppet, "I'm going to buy a new overcoat for my father, made of gold and silver, with diamond buttons; then I'll buy a Spelling Book."

"For yourself?"

"Of course. I'm going to go to school to work really hard."

"Look at me," said the Fox, "because of my foolish passion for study, I can't use my leg."

"And look at me," said the Cat, "because of *my* foolish passion for study, I am blind."

Just then a white blackbird perched in the hedgerow sang its usual song, then added: "Pinocchio, they're a bad lot, don't listen to them, take no notice, or you'll be sorry."

Poor blackbird, if only he hadn't said anything! The Cat leaped sky high and, without giving the bird a chance even to say *ouch*, swallowed him whole, feathers and all.

When he had devoured him and wiped his mouth, he shut his eyes, and was just as blind as before.

"Poor blackbird," said Pinocchio, "what did you do that for?"

"I did it for his own good. He must learn to mind his own business."

They were about half-way to Pinocchio's home when the Fox suddenly stopped and said: "Would you like to turn those five miserable gold pieces into a hundred, a thousand, or two thousand?"

"*Would* I? But how?"

"It's the easiest thing in the world. Come with us."

"Where to?"

"Cloud Cuckoo Land."

Pinocchio thought for a moment, and then said resolutely: "No, I won't. I'm almost home, my father is waiting to see me. He must be so worried."

"Think again, Pinocchio, you're turning your back on a fortune!"

"On a fortune!" repeated the Cat.

"Your five gold pieces might become two thousand in just one day!"

"But how could they possibly become so many?" demanded Pinocchio.

"I'll explain right now," said the Fox. "In Cloud Cuckoo Land there is a sacred place called the Field of Miracles. Here you dig a hole and put in it one gold coin. Then you cover it with earth, water it well with two buckets of spring water, sprinkle a pinch of salt over it, and go peacefully to bed.

"During the night the gold coin sprouts and blossoms and the next morning you get up, go back to the field, and what do you find? A lovely tree bowed down with gold coins!"

"So," said Pinocchio, more bewildered than ever, "if I bury my five gold pieces in that place, how many will there be in the morning?"

"That's easy," replied the Fox, "I can work it out on my fingers – two thousand five hundred shining, jingling gold pieces."

"Oh, how splendid!" cried Pinocchio, dancing for joy. "As soon as I have picked these gold pieces, I'll take two thousand for myself, and you two can have the remaining five hundred as a present."

"A present – for us?" exclaimed the Fox disdainfully. "What an insult! God forbid!"

"God forbid!" repeated the Cat.

"What good people!" thought Pinocchio; and straight away, he forgot his waiting father and all his good resolutions, and said to the Fox and Cat: "Well, lead on, I'll follow."

CHAPTER THIRTEEN
At the sign of the Red Crab

THEY WALKED, AND WALKED, and walked, and finally towards evening, tired out, they arrived at the Red Crab Inn.

"Let's stop here a while," said the Fox, "at least long enough to get a bite to eat, and rest a few hours. At midnight we must go on, so that we can reach the Field of Miracles by sunrise."

They went into the inn and sat down at one of the tables, but none of them had any appetite.

The poor Cat had a bad stomach ache and could only eat thirty-five sardines in tomato sauce, and four helpings of tripe with Parmesan cheese; and because he thought the tripe a little under-seasoned, he asked for three helpings of butter and grated cheese.

The Fox, too, would gladly have nibbled on some titbit but, as the doctor had put him on a strict diet, he had to make do with a hare in a sweet and sour sauce, surrounded by fat spring chickens. After the hare, in order to give himself a bit of an appetite, he ordered a dish of pheasants, partridges, rabbits, frogs, lizards, and Paradise grapes. After all this, he said he was sick of the sight of food and couldn't eat another mouthful.

Pinocchio ate least of all. He asked for a quarter of a nut, and a small crust from a loaf of dry bread, but he even left that on his plate. His thoughts were fixed on the Field of Miracles, and he was already suffering from indigestion from a surfeit of gold pieces.

When they had eaten, the Fox said to the innkeeper: "Give us two nice rooms: one for Master Pinocchio here, and the other for me and my companion. We'll take a little nap before we leave. Don't forget to call us at midnight, for we must continue our journey."

"Yes, sir," replied the innkeeper, winking at the Fox and Cat as if to say: "I understand what you two are up to."

As soon as he was in bed, Pinocchio fell fast asleep, and began to dream.

He dreamt he was in the middle of a field, and the field was full of little trees whose branches were bowed down with gold pieces, swinging gently in the breeze, all clinking and jingling, as if to say; 'Whoever wants us, come and get us.' But just at the most interesting part, when Pinocchio stretched out his hand to gather them in and put them in his pocket, he was suddenly woken by three violent knocks on his door.

It was the innkeeper to let him know it was midnight.

"Are my friends ready?" asked the puppet.

"Ready! They left two hours ago."

"Why were they in such a hurry?"

"The Cat received a message that his eldest son has chilblains and is not expected to live."

"Did they pay for their supper?"

"What an idea! They were far too polite to offer such an insult to a gentleman like yourself."

"That's too bad! That particular insult would have been most welcome!" said Pinocchio, scratching his head. Then he asked: "And where did my good friends say they would meet me?"

"In the Field of Miracles, tomorrow at sunrise."

Pinocchio paid the innkeeper a gold piece for the suppers, then left the Inn.

He had to feel his way, for it was so dark you couldn't see your hand in front of your face. Not a leaf could be heard stirring. Only a few night birds, flying across the path from one hedge to the other, brushed against Pinocchio's nose with their wings, making him start: "Who goes there?" they cried. There was an answering echo from the distant hills.

As he trudged along he saw a little creature on a tree trunk, which shone with a pale, faint light, like a night-light with a porcelain shade.

"Who are you?" asked Pinocchio.

"I'm the ghost of the Talking Cricket," was the reply that seemed to come from beyond the grave.

"What do you want with me?" said the puppet.

"I want to give you some advice. Go home, and take your four gold pieces to your father, who is missing you so much."

"This time tomorrow, my father will be a rich gentleman, for these four gold pieces will have become two thousand."

"Never trust people who promise to make you rich in a day. They're usually swindlers. Listen to me and go back home."

"No, I'm going on."

"It's very late. And it's very dark. And it's a dangerous road."

"I'm going on."

"Remember that children who do as they please regret it sooner or later."

"That's just an old wives' tale. Good night, Cricket!"

"Good night, Pinocchio; may Heaven preserve you from frogs and murderers."

With these words the Talking Cricket's light went out, and the path was darker than ever.

CHAPTER FOURTEEN

*Pinocchio meets
the murderers*

"REALLY IT'S TOO BAD," said the puppet to himself, as he continued his journey. "Children are so hard done by! Everybody scolds us, everybody warns us, everybody gives us advice. To hear them talk you'd think every adult is our father, or teacher – even a Talking Cricket has to chip in. It's absurd! Just because I won't listen to that tiresome Cricket. It's a good thing I don't believe in murderers. I'm positive that they were invented by parents on purpose just to frighten us, so that we won't go out at night. And just suppose I did meet them, I wouldn't be afraid! I'd walk right up to them and say: 'Now, Mr. Murderers, what do you want with me? You'd be foolish to do anything, you know. So shut up and mind your own business!' Hearing me talk like that, they'd just run like the wind. And if they didn't, then I would, and that would be the end of that."

Pinocchio was going to say something more, but he thought he heard leaves rustling behind him.

Turning quickly, he saw two horrid black figures wrapped in coal sacks leaping towards him, like two ghosts.

"It's them!" he said to himself, and not knowing what to do with his four gold pieces, he put them in his mouth, under his tongue.

Then he started to run; but before he had run a step, he felt his arms

36

seized, and heard two horrible, cavernous voices behind him.

"Your money or your life!" they cried, but Pinocchio couldn't speak because his money was in his mouth. He made a thousand bows and gestures to show these masked robbers that he was a poor man, and hadn't a penny in the world.

"Come, come, enough of that, hand over your money!" threatened the two swindlers.

But the puppet went on making signs with his head and hands.

"Hand over your money, or you're dead," said the tall murderer.

"Dead," repeated the other.

"And after we've killed you, we'll kill your father, too!"

"Your father, too!" repeated the other.

"No, no, no, not my father, no!" cried Pinocchio in despair; and the gold pieces jingled in his mouth.

"Ah, ah, you rascal, so you've hidden the money under your tongue! Spit it out, immediately!"

Pinocchio paid no attention.

"Oh! so you don't understand me? Wait a moment, we'll make you spit it out!"

One of the robbers seized the puppet by the end of his nose and the other grasped his chin, and then they pulled without mercy, this way and that, to make him open his mouth, but it was no use; it was as tightly shut as if it had been nailed together.

Then the smaller murderer drew a knife and tried to force it between Pinocchio's lips, but quick as lightning, Pinocchio bit off his hand. To his amazement he saw that it was a cat's paw!

He lost no time and jumped over the hedge and fled across the countryside with the murderers in hot pursuit, like dogs after a hare. The smaller one somehow ran on one leg.

After they had run about nine miles, Pinocchio was completely exhausted and lost so he climbed a tall pine tree and sat down on a branch at the very top. The murderers tried to follow him, but half-way up the trunk they slipped and fell to the ground, grazing their hands and feet.

In spite of this they did not give up, but lay a heap of dry sticks at the foot of the tree and set fire to it. In seconds the pine was blazing like a giant candle in the wind. Pinocchio, not wanting to be roasted like a chicken, leaped down from his perch and took to his legs again across the fields and vineyards. The murderers followed, running close behind him, never seeming to tire at all.

It was nearly daybreak and they were still running when, suddenly, Pinocchio found his way barred by a wide, deep ditch full of dirty water, the colour of milky coffee. What should he do? "One, two, three!" cried the puppet, and jumped clean over it. The murderers jumped too, but splash, spatter! They fell right into the middle of the ditch.

Pinocchio heard the splash, and as he ran he laughed, and shouted: "Enjoy a good bath, murderers!"

He was just thinking that they must have drowned when, turning to look, he saw them both running after him, still wrapped in their sacks, and dripping like two leaky baskets.

CHAPTER FIFTEEN

The murderers hang Pinocchio

Pinocchio was just about to surrender, when he saw a little house, as white as snow, far off among the dark green trees.

"If only I've breath enough to reach that house, perhaps I'll be safe," he said to himself.

Without losing a moment he ran towards the trees, as fast as he could, with the murderers hot on his tracks.

After running desperately for nearly two hours, he arrived at last, completely worn out, at the door of the little house.

He knocked; but no one answered.

He knocked again, louder than before, for he could hear the footsteps and the panting breath of his pursuers; but still no answer. He began to kick the door, and beat his head against it.

Just then a lovely young girl came to the window. Her hair was blue and her lovely face as white as wax; her eyes were closed, and her arms were crossed on her breast. Without moving her lips at all, she said in a low voice that seemed to come from the grave: "There is no one in this house. They are all dead."

"Let me in," cried Pinocchio, weeping and begging her.

"I'm dead, too."

"Dead? Then what are you doing at the window?"

"I'm waiting for the hearse to come and take me away."

As she said this the young girl disappeared, and the window closed.

"Oh, lovely blue-haired girl," implored Pinocchio, "open the door, for pity's sake. Have mercy on a poor boy who is being chased by murde . . ."

But before he could finish he felt himself grabbed by the neck, and heard those cruel voices snarling: "This time you won't escape us!" The puppet felt the end was near and he began to tremble. He shook so violently that the joints of his wooden legs creaked, and the four gold pieces under his tongue jingled.

"Now, then," demanded the murderers, "will you or will you not open your mouth? You won't answer, eh? Well, leave it to us: we'll see that you open it this time!"

And drawing out two razor-sharp knives, *slash, slash* . . . they struck out at him savagely. Lucky for him he was made of such hard wood that the blades splintered into a thousand pieces.

"I see there's no other way," said one of the wretches. "We must hang him!"

So they tied his hands behind his back, and putting a running noose around his neck, tied him to the branch of a big oak tree.

Then they sat down on the grass, and waited for him to stop kicking; but after three hours, the puppet's eyes were still open, and he was kicking as hard as ever, harder even.

At last, tired of waiting, they turned to Pinocchio and said with a sneer: "Good-bye, until tomorrow. Let's hope you'll oblige us and we'll find you good and dead, and with your mouth wide open."

With that they went away.

Meanwhile a fierce north wind began to blow, it raged and whistled, and blew poor Pinocchio backwards and forwards just like a church bell on a Sunday morning. It hurt him dreadfully and the noose tightened around his neck so much that he could not breathe.

Little by little his eyes grew dim and although he felt that death was near, he still hoped that a kind soul might rescue him. He waited and waited, but no one came. Then he remembered his poor father and half-dead he stammered: "Oh Father! If only you were here now!"

He could say no more. He closed his eyes, opened his mouth, stretched out his legs, shuddered all over, and then went as stiff as a board.

CHAPTER SIXTEEN

The lovely blue-haired girl
saves the puppet

WHILE POOR PINOCCHIO seemed more dead than alive, the lovely blue-haired girl looked out of the window again. She felt very sorry for him. She clapped her hands three times, making a faint sound.

At this signal there was a great rushing of wings, and a large Falcon appeared and perched on the windowsill.

"What is your command, beautiful Fairy?" said the Falcon, lowering his beak in homage (for the blue-haired girl was none other than a good fairy, who had lived near the woods for more than a thousand years).

"Do you see that puppet hanging from the big oak?"

"I see him."

"Very well, fly over there quickly; and with your strong beak break the knot that holds him, then lay him gently on the ground at the foot of the oak."

The Falcon flew away, and in two minutes he returned, saying: "Your orders have been obeyed."

"How did you find him? Alive or dead?"

"To look at him you'd think he's dead, but he can't be because as soon as I loosened the noose round his neck, he sighed and murmured: 'Now I feel better!'"

The Fairy clapped her hands twice, and a magnificent poodle appeared, walking upright on his hind legs, and dressed like a coachman on coronation day. He wore a little three-cornered hat trimmed with gold braid, a curly white wig, a chocolate-coloured doublet with diamond buttons and two great big pockets for the bones his mistress gave him every dinner-time. His short trousers were made of crimson velvet, and he wore silk stockings, low-heeled shoes and a sort of umbrella case behind, made of blue satin, this was to protect his tail when it rained.

"Be quick, Medoro!" said the Fairy. "Get out my finest carriage and drive to the woods. When you come to the big oak tree you'll find a half-dead puppet on the ground. Pick him up carefully, put him gently on the cushions, and bring him back to me. Do you understand?"

The Poodle was off like a shot.

In a few moments a magnificent carriage was driven out of the stable. It was the colour of pure air, and was upholstered in canary feathers and lined with whipped cream, custard and sweet biscuits. It was drawn by a hundred pairs of white mice. The Poodle on the box cracked his whip over their heads, he was in such a hurry.

In less than fifteen minutes he was back again. The Fairy was waiting at the door and took the puppet in her arms. She carried him into a little room with mother-of-pearl walls.

CHAPTER SEVENTEEN
Pinocchio tells a lie

THE FAIRY NURSED PINOCCHIO through a high fever. He was very stubborn and difficult about taking his medicine but she persuaded him that unless he took it he would not get better so, in the end, he swallowed the bitter dose, and soon was well again.

"Now tell me how you fell into the clutches of those murderers," the Fairy asked him.

"Well, Fire-Eater, the Showman, gave me some gold pieces and said: 'Here take these to your father.' But on the way I met Fox and Cat, two really nice characters, and they said: 'Would you like to change these four gold pieces into a thousand, or even two thousand? Come with us, and we'll take you to the Field of Miracles.'

"So I said: 'Let's go'; and they said: 'Let's stop at the Red Crab Inn, and set out again after midnight.'"

"And then I woke up and they'd gone away. I ran after them. It seemed impossibly dark, and I met two murderers in coal sacks, and they said: 'Hand over your money!' And I said: 'I haven't got any,' because I had hidden the gold pieces in my mouth. One of the murderers tried to put his hand in my mouth, and so I bit it off, and when I spat it out it had turned into a cat's paw. And the murderers ran after me, and I ran as fast as I could until they caught me, and hanged me by the neck from a big tree in the woods saying: 'We'll come back tomorrow, and then you'll be dead, and your mouth will be open, and we can get the money which is under your tongue.'"

"Where are the gold pieces now?" asked the Fairy.

"I've lost them," replied Pinocchio, but that was a lie because they were in his pocket.

As soon as he told this lie his nose, which was already very long, grew two inches longer.

"Where did you lose them?"

"In the woods, nearby."

His nose grew even longer.

"If you lost them there," said the Fairy, "we can go and look for them."

"Oh! Now I remember," replied the puppet getting flustered, "I didn't lose the money, I swallowed it when I was taking your medicine."

At this third lie his nose grew so long that poor Pinocchio couldn't move at all. If he turned one way, his nose hit the bed or the window, if he turned the other way, it hit the walls or the door; if he raised it, he was in danger of poking out the Fairy's eye.

The Fairy watched him and laughed.

"What are you laughing at?" asked the puppet, much embarrassed and worried by his enormous nose, which was growing all the time.

"I am laughing at the lies you have told me, little Pinocchio."

"However did you know that I had told lies?"

"Because lies are easily recognised. There are two sorts: those with short legs, and those with long noses. Your sort have long noses."

Pinocchio would have hidden his face in shame, had he been able to. He would have run out of the room but he couldn't reach the door, his nose was so long.

CHAPTER EIGHTEEN

*Pinocchio goes to plant his gold
pieces in the Field of Miracles*

IN ORDER TO TEACH him a lesson the Fairy let the puppet scream and cry a good half-hour. But when she saw his face all swollen from crying, and his eyes popping out of his head in despair, she was moved to pity. She clapped her hands once, and a thousand big woodpeckers flew in through the window, perched on Pinocchio's nose, and pecked away at it until it was back to its normal size.

"You're so kind, dear Fairy," said the puppet, "I love you so much!"

"I love you too," replied the Fairy, "and if you like you can stay here. You can be my little brother, and I will be your loving sister."

"I'd love to stay with you . . . but what about my poor father?"

"I've already thought of that. Your father knows all about you, he'll be here before nightfall."

"Really?" exclaimed Pinocchio jumping for joy. "Can we go and meet him. I can't wait to see him. He's suffered so much on my account!"

"Go, by all means, but don't get lost. Take the path through the wood, and you'll be sure to meet him."

Pinocchio left; and as soon as he reached the wood he ran like a deer. At the foot of the old oak tree, he stopped because he was sure he had heard a movement in the bushes. Who could it be? None other than the Fox and the Cat.

"Here's our dear friend Pinocchio," cried the Fox, giving him a big hug and a kiss. "What are you doing here?"

"What are you doing here?" repeated the Cat.

"It's a long story," said the puppet. "Two murderers hanged me from that tree."

And Pinocchio pointed to the big oak tree near by. "Did you ever!" said the Fox. "What a world we live in!"

While they were talking Pinocchio noticed that the Cat's right paw was missing. "Whatever's happened to your paw?" he asked.

The Cat began to stammer and Fox said quickly: "My friend is far too modest to tell you, so I will. About an hour ago we met an old wolf, who was almost dying of hunger, so what do you think my friend here did, he who has the heart of a king? He bit off his own paw and gave it to that poor beast so that he could have some breakfast."

As he said this, the Fox wiped away a tear. "And what are you doing here?" he asked.

"I'm waiting for my father; he should be here any minute now."

"And your gold pieces?"

"They're in my pocket, all except one, I spent that at the Red Crab Inn."

"Just think, instead of four gold pieces, you could have a thousand or even two thousand by tomorrow! Why not plant them in the Field of Miracles? Come with us. You could be there in half an hour and plant your four gold pieces, and after a few minutes you could pick up two thousand and go home with your pockets full. Won't you come?"

Pinocchio hesitated for a second; he thought about the good Fairy, and old Geppetto, and the warnings of the Talking Cricket; then he tossed his head and said to the Fox and Cat: "Come on, let's go."

And off they went.

They walked for about half a day until they came to Fools' Paradise. As soon as they entered the city, Pinocchio saw that the streets were full of dogs whose hair had all fallen out and whose mouths were gaping with hunger; there were shorn sheep, trembling with cold; chickens without their crests and combs, begging for a grain of corn; big butterflies who could not fly because they had sold their beautiful wings; peacocks without their tails, who were ashamed to be seen; and pheasants slinking along, mourning their lovely gold and silver feathers, which were lost for ever.

"But where is the Field of Miracles?" inquired Pinocchio.

"Just a few more steps."

They crossed the city, and once outside the walls, stopped in a lonely field, which looked just like any other field.

"Here we are," said the Fox. "Now get down and dig a little hole with your hands, and put in your gold pieces."

Pinocchio obeyed.

"Now then," said the Fox, "go to the mill-pond over there, and fetch a bucket of water and water the hole."

Pinocchio went to the mill-pond and took off his cap and then filled it with water, and came back to water his money.

"What else must I do?"

"Nothing," replied the Fox. "You can go now. Come back in about twenty minutes, and you'll find a little tree with branches laden with money."

Pinocchio was almost beside himself with joy.

The Fox and Cat wished Pinocchio a splendid harvest and left.

THE PUPPET WENT BACK to the city and began to count the minutes, one by one. When he thought he had waited twenty minutes, he hurried back to the Field of Miracles.

He ran as fast as he could. His heart beat like a drum, tum, tum, tum, tum, and he said to himself: "What if I find two thousand gold pieces on the tree instead of one thousand? Or instead of two thousand, five thousand? Or instead of five thousand, one hundred thousand? Oh, what a grand gentleman I should be then! I'd have a splendid palace with a thousand rocking horses and a thousand stables to play in, and a cellar full of toffee and lemonade, and a library crammed with candied fruit and jam tarts and swiss rolls, and marzipan and lollipops, and cream puffs!"

While he was indulging in these fantasies, he came within sight of the field. He stopped to see if he could catch a glimpse of a tree with its branches bowed down with money, but he saw nothing. He went a little further, still nothing. He walked into the field, right up to the place where he had planted his gold pieces, but there was nothing to be seen. He stood there thinking. Suddenly a loud laugh rang in his ears. Looking up he saw a large parrot on the branch of a tree, picking fleas off his last few feathers.

"Why are you laughing?" said Pinocchio peevishly.

"I'm laughing because I tickled myself under my wing."

The puppet did not reply. He went to the mill-pond, filled his cap with water again, and poured it on the earth which covered his money.

But another loud laugh, more mocking than ever, rang out over the lonely field.

"Look here," shouted Pinocchio angrily, "what are you laughing at, you bad-mannered parrot?"

"I'm laughing at those simpletons who believe all the nonsense they're told, and who're always cheated by those more cunning than themselves."

"Do you mean me?"

"Yes, Pinocchio, you're so idiotic you believe you can sow and reap money, just like beans or pumpkins. I believed that too, once, and look at me now!

"I learned too late that to get a little money together, honestly, you must work for it by the sweat of your brow, or, by using your brains."

"I don't understand what you mean," said the puppet, beginning to tremble.

"I'll try to explain," replied the parrot. "While you were in the city, the Fox and the Cat came back here and dug up your money and ran away like the wind. It would take a marathon runner to catch them now."

Pinocchio just stood there with his mouth wide open in disbelief. Wildly, he dug and dug and dug, until he had made a hole as big as a house, but the money was not there.

Then, in desperation, he ran back to the city and went straight to the Court House to denounce the swindlers.

The judge was a Gorilla. He was very old indeed, and looked very respectable. He had a long white beard and bad eyes so he wore gold spectacles, without any lenses in them.

In the judge's presence Pinocchio described in minute detail how he had been cheated, and demanded justice.

The judge listened compassionately, for he was really interested in Pinocchio's story, and felt very sorry for him. Then he rang a bell and two mastiffs appeared, dressed as policemen.

The judge pointed to Pinocchio and said: "This poor fellow has been robbed of four gold pieces. Arrest him, and take him to prison immediately."

Pinocchio was thunderstruck. He was about to protest but the policemen didn't waste any time, they clapped their paws over his mouth and took him to prison.

And there he stayed for four long months and it would have been longer if the young emperor of Fools' Paradise hadn't won a great victory over his enemies, and ordered a celebration. There were illuminations, fireworks, horse and bicycle races, and, best of all, the prison gates were thrown open and everyone was set free.

CHAPTER TWENTY

Pinocchio is caught in a man-trap

PINOCCHIO WAS OVERJOYED to be free again! He hurried out of the city, and set off for the Fairy's house.

It had been raining hard, and the mud was so deep that it came up to his knees; but he ignored it. He was so looking forward to seeing his father and the Fairy that he ran and jumped like a greyhound until the mud splashed and spattered as high as his head.

He had to reach the Fairy's house before dark. But he was severely delayed by a serpent blocking his path and when he was free to go on he was so dreadfully hungry that he jumped over a hedge to pick a few bunches of grapes.

He had barely reached the vine, when SNAP! he felt his legs gripped by two sharp irons: the pain was so terrible that he saw stars. The puppet was caught in a man-trap, laid to catch the polecats who terrorised all the chicken-coops in the neighbourhood.

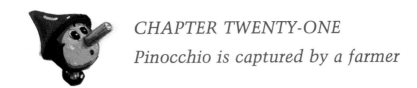

PINOCCHIO BEGAN TO scream and cry and call for help; but in vain, for there were no houses to be seen, and not a living soul passed by.

Meanwhile it grew dark.

Pinocchio was almost fainting from the pain of the cruel irons, which cut into his shins, and because he was so afraid, all alone in the dark in the middle of the fields. Then he saw a firefly above his head, and called to him: "Oh, little Firefly, have mercy on me. Help!"

"Poor boy!" replied the Firefly, gazing at him compassionately. "How on earth did you get caught?"

"I wanted to pick some grapes and . . ."

"Hunger is no excuse for taking what doesn't belong to you."

"That's true, that's true," wailed Pinocchio, "I won't do it again."

Their conversation was interrupted by the sound of footsteps. The owner of the field was approaching on tiptoe to see if he had caught a polecat.

When he drew his lantern from under his coat he was amazed to see that, instead of a polecat, he had caught a little boy.

"Ah, you thief!" the farmer said angrily, "so it's you who're stealing my chickens!"

"It isn't me, it isn't me," sobbed Pinocchio; "I only came into the field to eat a few grapes!"

"Anyone who steals grapes will steal chickens, too. I'll teach you a lesson you'll never forget."

He opened the man-trap, seized the puppet by the collar, and lugged him off like a stray lamb.

When he reached the farmyard near the house, he threw Pinocchio to the ground, and putting one foot on his neck, said: "It's late, and I want to go to bed. I'll settle your hash tomorrow. My guard dog died today. For the time being, you can take his place."

So without further ado, he fastened a heavy collar covered with sharp brass studs round Pinocchio's neck, so tightly that he couldn't possibly slip his head through it. A long iron chain was attached to the collar, and fixed firmly to the wall.

"If it rains tonight," said the farmer, "you can sleep in that kennel. The straw in there hasn't been changed for four years. Remember to keep your ears pricked, and, if the thieves come, don't forget to bark."

With this last warning, the farmer went into the house.

CHAPTER TWENTY-TWO
Pinocchio is set free

HE HAD BEEN SLEEPING soundly for two hours, when at about midnight he was woken up by whispering and mutterings that seemed to be coming from the yard. He poked his nose out of the kennel and saw four dark furry animals talking to each other. They looked like cats, but they were polecats, and are especially fond of eggs and young chickens. One of them came to the door of the kennel and said in a low tone: "Good evening, Lightning."

"My name isn't Lightning," said the puppet.

"Who are you then?"

"I'm Pinocchio."

"And what are you doing here?"

"I'm a guard dog."

"But where's Lightning?"

"He died this morning."

"Died? Poor beast! He was so kind! However, judging by your face you also seem to be a good-natured dog."

"Excuse me, but I'm not a dog! I'm a puppet."

"And you're a guard puppet?"

"I'm afraid so: I'm being punished!"

"Well, I'll make the same deal with you as I made with old Lightning; I'm sure you'll be satisfied. We'll come to the chicken-coop one night a week, as usual, and take eight hens. We'll eat seven, and give you one, on one condition – you must pretend to be asleep when we come, and never bark and wake up the farmer."

Pinocchio assured the creature that he understood.

When the four pole-cats were sure it was safe, they went straight to the chicken-coop. They tore open the little wooden door with their teeth and claws, and had no sooner slipped inside when the door closed with a loud bang.

Pinocchio had closed it, and not only that, he had put a large stone against it to make sure the polecats were trapped.

Then he began to bark.

When the farmer heard him, he jumped out of bed, seized his gun, and called out of the window: "What's the matter?"

"The thieves are here!" cried Pinocchio.

"Where?"

"In the chicken-coop!"

"I'm coming right down."

In a flash the farmer appeared. He ran to the chicken-coop, and after catching the four polecats and popping them into a sack, he exclaimed, happily, "At last I have you!"

Then he went up to Pinocchio, and stroked and patted him, and asked: "However did you discover their plot? To think that faithful old Lightning never suspected anything!"

Pinocchio told the farmer but without betraying Lightning – let him rest in peace.

"Good for you, my boy," said the farmer, patting him on the back. "To show how pleased I am with you, I'll set you free, and send you home."

And, with that, he took off the dog collar.

CHAPTER TWENTY-THREE

Pinocchio weeps for the death
of the Fairy

WITHOUT THE WEIGHT of that heavy, humiliating collar round his neck, Pinocchio began to run across the fields, never stopping for a moment, until he reached the field where the little white house had stood. But it was no longer there. Instead there was a little slab of pure white marble on which these sad words were inscribed:

> HERE LIES
> THE BLUE-HAIRED FAIRY
> WHO DIED OF GRIEF
> ON BEING ABANDONED
> BY HER LITTLE
> BROTHER PINOCCHIO

Pinocchio's heart almost broke when he had spelled out these words. He fell to the ground, and kissing the cold marble a thousand times, he burst into a flood of tears. He wept all that night.

"Now that I've lost you and my father, who will feed me? Where will I sleep? Who will make me a new coat? I think I'd be better off dead. I want to die! Boo-hoo-hoo!" he sobbed.

Pinocchio tried to tear out his hair, but since it was made of wood he couldn't even run his fingers through it.

At this moment a very large Dove, flying high above him, suddenly stopped in mid-flight with outstretched wings, and cried: "Tell me, do you happen to know a puppet called Pinocchio?"

"Pinocchio?" cried the puppet, jumping to his feet. "I'm Pinocchio!"

At this reply the Dove dropped swiftly to the ground. He was larger than a turkey.

"Do you know Geppetto?" he asked the puppet.

"Do I know him? He's my father! Has he spoken about me to you? Is he still alive?"

"I left him on the seashore three days ago. He was making a little boat in which to cross the ocean. That poor man! For the last four months he's been wandering the earth looking for you."

"How far is it from here to the seashore?" Pinocchio inquired anxiously.

"More than five hundred miles."

"Oh, if only I had your wings!"

"If you want to go I'll carry you."

"How?"

"On my back. Are you very heavy?"

"No, I'm as light as a feather!"

Without another word Pinocchio jumped astride the Dove's back, and cried out joyfully: "Gallop, gallop, little horse, I'm in a hurry!"

The Dove took flight, and in a few minutes was so high up that he almost touched the clouds. Pinocchio couldn't help looking down at the world below him; but it frightened him, and made him so dizzy that he wound his arms tightly around the Dove's neck to stop himself from falling off.

They flew all day. Towards evening the Dove said: "I'm so thirsty."

"And I'm so hungry!" added Pinocchio.

"Let's stop at this dovecote for a few minutes then we can continue our journey, and by sunrise we should be at the seashore."

They entered the deserted dovecote where they found only a basin of water and a basket of lettuce.

Pinocchio always said lettuce turned his stomach; but that evening he devoured it.

Next morning they were at the seashore. The Dove stopped just long enough for Pinocchio to dismount, and then flew off because he couldn't bear to be thanked.

The beach was crowded with people shouting and pointing as they looked out over the ocean.

"What's the matter?" Pinocchio asked a little old woman.

"A poor father has lost his son and he is about to cross the sea in a little boat to look for him, but the waves are so high, the boat is bound to sink . . . Look, follow my finger," she said, pointing to a little boat, which at that distance looked like a nutshell with a tiny man in it.

Pinocchio looked closely, and uttered a piercing shriek: "It's my father! It's my father!"

Meanwhile the little boat, beaten by the angry waves, disappeared entirely, and then re-appeared on the crest of a wave. Pinocchio, standing on a high rock, called his father's name over and over again, making signs with his hands, and waving his cap and handkerchief.

Although Geppetto was so far away, it seemed as if he recognised his son, for he took off his cap and waved it: he also made signs to show that he would gladly return to land, but the sea was so savage that he could not use his oars.

Suddenly a mighty wave rose, and the little boat disappeared for ever.

"The poor man!" said the fishermen on the beach; and murmuring a prayer they turned away to go back home.

Suddenly there was a desperate shout, and turning round to look they saw a boy throw himself into the sea from the top of a high rock, shouting: "I will save my father!"

Pinocchio, being made of wood, floated easily and swam like a fish. They saw him disappear under the water and reappear only to be beaten about by the waves. At last, they lost sight of him altogether.

"Poor boy!" said the fishermen and murmuring another prayer.

CHAPTER TWENTY-FOUR

Pinocchio arrives at
Busy-Bee Island

HOPING TO ARRIVE in time to save his father, Pinocchio swam all that night, through floods of rain, hailstones, terrible thunderclaps, and flashes of lightning that turned the dark world to day.

Towards morning he saw, not far off, a long strip of land. It was an island in the midst of the ocean. He tried as hard as he could to reach the shore, but all in vain. The tumbling waves tossed him backwards and forwards as if he were a piece of straw. At last, luck was with him, a gigantic wave picked him up and threw him violently on to the beach.

Little by little the clouds disappeared, the sun shone forth in all its splendour, and the sea became as smooth as a mill-pond.

The puppet sat on the beach to dry in the sun and scanned that vast ocean for a little boat with an old man in it. But he looked in vain.

Pinocchio was just about to cry when he saw a large fish close to the shore, swimming with its head out of the water.

Since he didn't know its name, he shouted at the top of his voice: "Hello, Master Fish, may I have a word with you?"

"You may have two words if you like," replied the fish who was really a very polite Dolphin. In fact in all the seas and oceans he was unique.

"Will you please tell me if there are places on this island where one may eat, without being eaten?"

"There is one just a short distance from here," replied the Dolphin.

"How do I get there?"

"Take that little path on your left, and follow your nose, you can't go wrong."

"Please tell me one more thing. You swim in the sea day and night: have you by any chance seen a little boat with my father in it?"

"Who's your father?"

"He's the best father in all the world; and I'm the worst son."

"After last night's storm," said the Dolphin, "his boat was probably sunk."

"And my father?"

"By now he must have been eaten by the terrible shark that has been spreading death and destruction in these waters for a long time."

"Is this shark very big?" inquired Pinocchio, trembling with fright.

"Is he big?" exclaimed the Dolphin. "Well, just to give you an idea, he's taller than a five-storey house, and his mouth is so wide and deep that it would easily hold a train-engine, carriages and all."

"Heavens above!" cried the terrified puppet and, turning to the Dolphin said: "Good-bye, Master Fish, sorry for any trouble I've caused you, and a thousand thanks."

At the slightest sound he quickly turned to look behind him, terrified in case the shark was after him.

About half an hour later, he came to Busy-Beeville. The streets were full of bustling people; everybody had something to do; everybody was working; you couldn't find one idle layabout or tramp. Meanwhile, Pinocchio had decided: "This place won't do for me. I wasn't born to work."

By this time he was famished. There were only two ways of getting something to eat: to ask for work, or to beg for a few pennies or a bit of bread. He was ashamed to beg. His father had always taught him that only the aged, the sick and the helpless have the right to beg, because they can no longer work to earn their living. Everyone else has to work; and if they refuse to, and are hungry, so much the worse for them.

While Pinocchio hesitated, a man passed by, perspiring and panting. With great difficulty, he was pulling two carts loaded with coal.

Pinocchio decided that he had a kind face; so he went up to him, and casting down his eyes in shame, he said in a low voice: "Will you give me a penny, please. I'm dying of hunger."

"I'll give you four pennies," replied the coal-man, "if you'll help me pull these loads of coal home."

"Certainly not!" exclaimed the puppet indignantly. "For your information, I'm not a donkey!"

"Good for you!" replied the coal-man. "Then, my boy, if you are really hungry, eat a couple of slices of your pride, and be careful not to get indigestion."

In the next half-hour, twenty people passed by, and Pinocchio begged from every one of them, but they all replied: "Aren't you ashamed! Instead of begging on the streets, go to work and earn your bread!"

At last a kind little woman appeared carrying two pitchers of water.

"Please, madam, will you let me have a sip of water from your pitcher?" asked Pinocchio, who was burning with thirst.

"Yes, drink, my child," said the little woman.

When Pinocchio had drunk deeply, and was as full as a wet sponge, he wiped his mouth and grumbled: "Now I'm no longer thirsty! If only I were no longer hungry!"

"If you carry one of these pitchers for me, I'll give you a slice of bread."

Pinocchio looked at the heavy pitcher and hesitated.

"And as well as the bread I'll give you a dish of tasty pickled cauliflower," the good woman added.

Pinocchio looked at the pitcher again, and still he hesitated.

"After the cauliflower I'll give you some delicious cake."

Pinocchio could resist no longer; he drew a long breath and said resolutely: "All right! I'll carry the pitcher home for you."

The pitcher was very heavy, and the puppet's hands weren't strong enough to carry it so he put it on his head.

When they arrived at her home the good woman placed Pinocchio at a little table already set, and gave him the bread, and the cauliflower, and the cake.

Pinocchio ate like a pig. His stomach was like a house that had been empty for months.

Little by little the worst pangs of hunger were satisfied and he raised his head to thank his benefactress. No sooner had he looked at her than he uttered a long drawn out "O-o-o-o-o-h!" of astonishment.

"Whatever's the matter with you?" said the good woman, laughing.

"It's because . . ." stammered Pinocchio, "it's because . . . because . . . you're like . . . you remind me . . . you have blue hair too, just like her! Oh dear Fairy, oh dear Fairy, tell me, is it you? Is it really you? Don't make me cry any more! If only you knew how much I've suffered."

Pinocchio wept floods of tears and, falling on to his knees, he threw his arms round the mysterious little woman.

CHAPTER TWENTY-FIVE

Pinocchio makes the Fairy
a promise

AT FIRST THE LITTLE woman would not admit that she was the Fairy; but when she knew that Pinocchio had recognised her and not wanting to tease Pinocchio any longer, she said: "You naughty puppet, how did you recognise me?"

"Because I love you so much."

"I was a young girl when you left me and now I'm old enough to be your mother."

"But that's wonderful. I've always wanted a mother like real boys have. But how did you grow up so quickly?"

"That's a secret."

"Tell me: I'd like to be a little taller. Just look at me! I've never been more than knee-high."

"But you can't grow," replied the Fairy.

"Why not?"

"Because puppets never grow."

"I'm sick to death of being a puppet!" cried Pinocchio, banging his wooden head. "It's about time I became a man!"

"If only you deserved it, you could be one."

"Really? And what do I have to do to deserve that?"

"It's very easy: you begin by being a good boy and doing as you're told, telling the truth and going to school."

"Right, from today I'll turn over a new leaf," Pinocchio announced.

"Do you promise?"

"Yes, I promise. I want to be a good boy and make my father happy. Where can he be?"

"I don't know."

"Will I ever see him again?"

"I hope so; yes, I'm sure you will."

Pinocchio was so happy when he heard this that he grasped the Fairy's hands and kissed them. Then looking up at her affectionately, he asked: "It wasn't true, then, that you were dead? If only you knew how sad I was."

"I know, and that's why I forgave you. You were really sorry, and I knew that you had a good heart; and if a child has a good heart, even if he's mischievous and badly brought up, one can always hope he'll mend his ways. That's why I came here to look for you. I will be your mother . . ."

"Oh, how wonderful!" shouted Pinocchio, jumping for joy.

"You must always obey me and do as you're told."

"Oh, yes, yes, yes!"

"Tomorrow," added the Fairy, "you will begin by going to school."

Pinocchio was not pleased.

"What are you muttering about?" inquired the Fairy indignantly.

"I was saying," grumbled Pinocchio, "that it seems too late for me to go to school now."

"No it isn't. It's never too late to get an education."

"But I don't want to learn a profession or a trade . . ."

"Why not?"

"Because I don't like work."

"Dear Pinocchio," said the Fairy, "people who talk like that end up in a hospital or a prison or worse. Every man, whether he's born rich or poor, has to find something to do in this world – to keep himself busy."

Pinocchio's heart was touched at last. He lifted up his head quickly and said to the Fairy: "I *will* study, I *will* work. I'll do everything you want, for I'm really sick of being a puppet. I want to be a real boy, whatever the cost. You promised, didn't you?"

"Yes, I promised, and now it's up to you."

CHAPTER TWENTY-SIX

*Pinocchio goes to see
the terrible shark*

THE VERY NEXT DAY Pinocchio went to school. When the other children saw a puppet in school they laughed and laughed. Then the fun began. They tried to draw an ink moustache on his upper lip, and finally, they tried to tie strings to his hands and feet to make him dance.

At first Pinocchio pretended not to notice them, but at last he lost his temper, and threatened them: "Be careful or else!"

The rudest one of them all tried to grab Pinocchio by the nose. But he was not quite quick enough, for Pinocchio kicked his shins under the table.

"Ouch! What hard feet!" cried the boy, rubbing his aching shins.

"And what sharp elbows! They're harder than his feet!" shrieked the boy who'd received a blow in the pit of his stomach in return for his unkind jokes.

By showing he could defend himself, Pinocchio won the respect and goodwill of the whole school, and everyone grew very fond of him.

Even the teacher praised him, because he was attentive, hard-working, and intelligent. He always arrived first and was the last to leave.

His only fault was that he made too many friends, and some of them were trouble-makers. The teacher warned him about them every day, so did the Fairy.

One day, on his way to school he met one of these trouble-makers, who said: "Have you heard the news?"

"No."

"They say there's a shark in the sea as big as a mountain."

"Is there really? Perhaps it's the same shark that I heard about the night my poor father was drowned?"

"We're going to the beach to see it. Are you coming, too?"

"No! I'm going to school."

"What's the point? We can go to school tomorrow. What's one lesson more or less? We'll still be as dim."

"I know what I'll do," said Pinocchio, "I must see that shark, but I'll go after school."

"You idiot!" replied one of the boys. "Do you think a fish that size will wait until you see fit to call on it?"

"How long will it take to get to the beach?" asked the puppet.

"We can be there and back in an hour."

"Well, come on then, last one there's a tortoise!" cried Pinocchio.

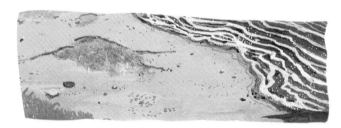

CHAPTER TWENTY-SEVEN
Pinocchio is arrested

WHEN HE ARRIVED AT the seashore, Pinocchio looked round quickly, but he could not see a shark. The sea was as smooth as a great mirror.

"Well, where's the shark?" he inquired, turning to his companions.

"Perhaps he's having breakfast," said one of them, laughing.

"Or maybe he's gone to bed for a nap," said another, laughing still louder.

Pinocchio realised that it was all a joke.

"Why did you tell me about the shark?"

"We wanted you to play truant with us. You make all of us look even worse in the eyes of our teacher. Be like us, hate school, and lessons, and the teacher: they're our three greatest enemies."

"And just suppose I go on as usual?"

"Then we'll have nothing more to do with you and, as soon as we can, we'll get even with you!"

"You make me laugh," said the puppet, shaking his head.

"Be careful, Pinocchio," said one of the biggest of the boys as he walked towards him. "Don't think you can bully us. Remember you're alone here and there're seven of us!"

"Seven, like the seven deadly sins," exclaimed Pinocchio, laughing bravely.

"Did you hear that? He's insulted us, he called us the seven deadly sins!"

"Say you're sorry, Pinocchio, or it'll be all the worse for you!"

"Cuckoo!" said the puppet, tapping his nose derisively.

"You'll be sorry, Pinocchio."

"Cuckoo!"

"We'll beat you like a dog!"

"Cuckoo!"

"I'll give you 'Cuckoo!"cried the most daring of the bullies. "Put this in your pipe and smoke it."

With this he punched him on the head. But Pinocchio replied with another punch, and then they were all fighting furiously. Pinocchio defended himself like a hero.

Then because they couldn't get near Pinocchio, the boys began to throw things at him. First they threw their books. But Pinocchio dodged so quickly that all the books flew over his head and into the sea.

The fish thought the books were food, and came to the surface in shoals; but no sooner had they tasted a page or two than they spat it out again with a grimace which seemed to say: "We're used to better food than that, thank you!"

Then the boys saw the puppet's books lying on the ground, and grabbed them.

Among them was a large *Treatise on Arithmetic*, bound in leather, with leather spine and corners. It was extremely heavy.

One of the boys picked it up and aiming at Pinocchio's head, let fly with all the force he could muster: but instead of hitting the puppet it struck one of his friends on the head.

The child turned as white as a sheet and crying out, "Mother, help me, I'm dying!" he fainted.

The frightened boys took to their heels and in a few seconds were out of sight. But Pinocchio stayed behind and although he was more dead than alive with sorrow and fright, he soaked a handkerchief in the sea and put it on the boy's temples. He wept and shouted: "Eugene, Eugene! Open your eyes and look at me! Why don't you answer me? It wasn't me, honest, it wasn't me! Open your eyes, Eugene. If you don't, I'll die too. How can I go back home now? Where can I hide? Oh, if only I'd gone to school! Why did I listen to these boys? I always do as I please! And afterwards I always pay for it."

Suddenly he heard footsteps. He turned. There were two policemen.

"What are you doing on the ground?" they demanded.

"I was helping my friend."

"This boy has been struck on the temple; who did it?"

"Not me," stammered Pinocchio, who was so frightened he could hardly breathe.

"If it wasn't you, who was it then?"

"Not me," repeated Pinocchio.

"What caused it?"

"This book."

The puppet picked up the *Treatise on Arithmetic* and showed it to the policemen.

"Whose book's this?"

"Mine."

"That's good enough. I don't need to hear any more. Get up, and come with us."

"But I . . ."

"Come along!"

"But I'm innocent . . ."

"Come along!"

They found a fisherman to look after Eugene. Then placing Pinocchio between them, they ordered him to "Forward march! and step lively! If you don't . . . so much the worse for you, my lad!"

So the puppet, terribly ashamed, started down the path that led to the village. Poor little Pinocchio didn't know whether he was dreaming or what. One thought pierced his heart like a sword: he would have to pass under the Fairy's window escorted by two policemen. He would rather die.

They were just entering the village when a gust of wind carried Pinocchio's cap away.

"May I fetch my cap, please?" Pinocchio asked the policemen.

"All right, but be quick about it."

The puppet picked up his cap but instead of placing it on his head, he bit on it and ran for the sea.

The policemen sent Goldenwing, a great mastiff to catch him. Goldenwing was a champion runner!

CHAPTER TWENTY-EIGHT

*Pinocchio is in danger of being
fried like a fish*

DURING THIS TERRIBLE race, there was a moment when Pinocchio felt all was lost, for Goldenwing had almost caught him. Luckily, by this time, Pinocchio was only a few steps from the sea. And in he plunged.

Goldenwing would have stopped, but he was going too fast and he shot out into the sea. When he came to the surface his eyes were almost starting out of his head. He barked and yelped: "I'm drowning! I'm drowning!"

"Drown then," replied Pinocchio, who was safe now.

"Help me, Pinocchio, save me!"

At that cry of despair the puppet took pity on him, and turning to the dog, he said: "If I save your life, will you promise not to bother me or run after me any more?"

"I promise! I promise! Be quick! Another second, and I'll be drowned."

Pinocchio hesitated an instant, but he remembered how his father had told him so many times that one should always try and do a good deed. He swam to Goldenwing, and taking his tail in both hands, he pulled him safe and sound to dry land.

The poor dog couldn't stand up; he had drunk so much salt water that he was like a balloon. However, the puppet didn't quite trust him, so he left him on the beach. As he swam away he called back to him: "Good-bye, Goldenwing, have a nice trip, and give my love to everyone."

"Good-bye, Pinocchio," replied the dog. "You've done me a great kindness, and in this world, one good turn deserves another. If you should ever need me, I'll be there."

Pinocchio swam on but he kept close to the shore until at last he thought he had found a safe place. On the beach he saw a kind of grotto carved out of the rock, and a long column of smoke pouring out of it.

"There must be a fire in that grotto," he said to himself. "So much the better! I can dry myself and then? Well, we'll see."

So he swam towards the rocks. But as he was climbing out, he felt something rising from below the surface of the water, rising, rising, until it

lifted him right up and out on to the beach. He tried to run away but it was too late. He was caught in a huge net, and was surrounded by a multitude of fish of every size and shape. They were all flapping and jumping about as if they were crazy.

And then he saw a terrifying fisherman coming out of the grotto. He was so ugly he looked like a sea monster. Instead of hair, a bush thickly covered with green leaves grew on his head. His skin was green, his eyes were green, and his long beard that almost touched the ground, was also green. He looked like a great green lizard standing on its hind legs.

When the Green Fisherman had drawn the net out of the sea, he cried out joyfully: "Praise be! I shall have a lovely fish dinner today, too!"

"It's lucky for me I'm not a fish," said Pinocchio to himself.

The net full of fish was carried into the grotto. It was dark and smoky and in the middle there was a big frying-pan full of hot oil, which smelled like a snuffed-out candle, and nearly took your breath away.

"Now let's see what sort of fish we have here!" said the Green Fisherman.

The last one out of the net was Pinocchio.

When the Green Fisherman pulled him out, he opened his green eyes wide in astonishment and cried out, almost in a panic: "What sort of fish do we have here? I've never eaten one like this before!"

After turning him over and over, and examining him carefully, he said: "It must be a sea-crab."

"How dare you call me a crab? What an insult! I am a puppet!"

"A puppet?" said the Green Fisherman. "To tell you the truth, a puppet-fish is new to me. All the better! I shall eat you with even greater pleasure!"

"Eat *me*? Can't you see that I'm not a fish? Don't you see that I can talk and reason, just like you?"

"That's very true, so I will treat you with great consideration. It's not every day that one catches a puppet-fish. Leave it to me. I think I'll fry you in the pan with all the other fish. You'll be perfectly happy."

Pinocchio wept and screamed and begged for mercy. But the Green Fisherman took a reed, and after binding him hand and foot like an Italian sausage, he threw him into the tub with the others.

Pinocchio could only implore with his eyes; but the Green Fisherman, without so much as a glance, rolled him five or six times in the flour, and covered him so completely that he looked like a chalk puppet.

Then he took him by the head and . . .

JUST AS THE GREEN Fisherman was about to drop Pinocchio into the frying-pan, a large dog came into the grotto.

"Get out!" threatened the Green Fisherman, still holding the floury puppet in his hand.

But the dog was so hungry he was determined to stay, and he growled at the Green Fisherman, showing a row of sharp teeth.

Just then he heard a faint little voice: "Save me, Goldenwing, I'm going to be fried!"

The dog recognised Pinocchio's voice at once and jumped high in the air, seized the bundle and holding it carefully between his teeth, ran out of the grotto and away like the wind.

When Goldenwing came to the path that led to the village, he stopped and put Pinocchio down gently.

"How can I ever thank you?" said the puppet.

"You needn't thank me," replied the dog. "You saved my life and one good turn deserves another."

Goldenwing held out his right paw to Pinocchio, who squeezed it hard as a sign of friendship, and then they parted.

As he walked along, Pinocchio began to feel a little uneasy. He took one step forward, then one back, and said to himself: "How can I face the Fairy? What will she say when she sees me? Will she forgive me a second time? I'm sure she won't. And it serves me right. I always promise to do better, but I never keep my word."

He arrived in the village after dark, and because it was a stormy night, and the rain was pouring down in bucketfuls, he went straight to the Fairy's house, to ask for shelter.

But when he came to the door he was afraid to knock, and ran away; he tried again and again but he still couldn't bring himself to knock.

The fourth time he took hold of the iron knocker and let it fall very lightly, trembling as he did so. He waited and waited, and at last, after half an hour, a window on the fourth floor at the top of the house was thrown open and a big Snail with a tiny light on its head looked out, and said: "Who's there, at this hour of the night?"

"Is the Fairy at home?" asked Pinocchio.

"The Fairy is asleep and doesn't want to be disturbed! Who are you?"

"It's me."

"Me? Who's me?"

"Pinocchio."

"Who's Pinocchio?"

"The puppet who lives with the Fairy."

"Ah! I see," said the Snail, "wait for me, I'll be right down to open the door."

"Please hurry, I'm dying of cold!"

"I am a Snail, and Snails are never in a hurry."

An hour passed, two hours, and still the door was not opened; so Pinocchio, who was shaking with cold and fright and damp, plucked up enough courage to knock once more, this time a little louder.

A window opened on the third floor, and the same Snail looked out.

"Kind Snail," cried Pinocchio, "I've been waiting two hours! And two hours in this horrid weather is like two years. Please, please hurry!"

"My child," said the Snail, "I am a Snail and Snails are never in a hurry."

And the window on the third floor shut tight.

Not long afterwards the village clock struck midnight; then one, then two o'clock, and the door was still closed.

Finally, Pinocchio lost his temper. He grabbed the knocker and was about to make the whole house shake when, suddenly, the iron knocker turned into a live eel, slipped out of his hands and disappeared in the rivulets of rain water that were running in the streets.

"Right then!" shouted Pinocchio, boiling over with rage, "if the door knocker has run away, I'll kick the door down!"

And drawing back, he let fly a furious kick and his foot

went clean through the door and when he tried to pull his foot back, he couldn't. His foot was stuck in the door, just as if it had been nailed in.

Pinocchio spent the rest of the night with one foot on the ground, and the other through the door.

Finally, at daybreak, the door was opened. That obliging Snail had taken only nine hours to come down from the fourth floor to the street door!

"What are you doing with your foot sticking through the door?" she inquired, laughing.

"It was an accident. Could you please find a way of freeing me from my torment?"

"This is a job for a carpenter and I've never been a carpenter."

"Please ask the Fairy to help."

"The Fairy doesn't want to be disturbed."

"But what am I going to do all day, nailed to this door?"

"You can amuse yourself by counting the passing ants."

"At least bring me something to eat, I'm fainting with hunger."

"Immediately!" said the Snail.

In fact, three and a half hours later Pinocchio saw her coming back with a tray on her head. There was bread, a roast chicken, and four ripe apricots.

'Here's your breakfast, with the Fairy's compliments," said the Snail.

At the sight of all that food, the puppet was quite consoled. But when he began to eat, he discovered that the bread was made out of plaster, the chicken out of papier mâché, and the four apricots were alabaster, all painted to look real.

He felt like weeping, throwing the tray and everything on it far away, instead he fainted.

When he came to, the Fairy was bending over him.

"I will forgive you just once more," said the Fairy, "but woe betide you if you do wrong again."

Pinocchio promised and solemnly vowed he would work hard at school and always be good; and he kept his word for the whole year. He did well and passed all his examinations with flying colours. The Fairy was very pleased with him and said: "Tomorrow, I'll grant your wish and you will turn into a real live boy."

No one who wasn't there could possibly imagine Pinocchio's joy at hearing this. All his friends and the whole class were to be invited to come to the Fairy's house, next day, to celebrate the wonderful event with a special breakfast.

The day promised to be so happy but . . .

CHAPTER THIRTY
Pinocchio listens to Shoelace

PINOCCHIO ASKED the Fairy's permission to go round the village and invite his friends to the celebration. She said: "Of course, go and invite all your friends, but remember to come home before dark."

"I promise to be back in an hour," said the puppet.

The puppet gave the Fairy a big kiss and ran out of the house singing and dancing.

In less than an hour he had invited all his friends.

Now Pinocchio had one very special friend. His name was Romeo, but everybody called him by his nickname, 'Shoelace', because he was so thin and long and floppy. He looked just like a shoelace.

Shoelace was the laziest and the most mischievous boy in the school, but Pinocchio thought a great deal of him. In fact, he went to his home first of all, but he wasn't there. He went back twice but Shoelace was still not there.

Pinocchio found him at last, hiding under the porch of a farmer's house. "What on earth are you doing here?" Pinocchio asked as he crawled under the porch to join him.

"I'm waiting for midnight, then I'm going away."

"Where are you going?"

"Far, far away from here. I'm going to live in a place – the most beautiful place in the world – a perfect paradise!"

"What's this place called?"

"Toyland. Why don't you come, too?"

"Me? Me, never!"

"You're making a big mistake, Pinocchio! If you don't come I know you'll regret it. Where could you find a better place for us boys? In Toyland there are no schools, no teachers, and no books. No one ever studies."

"But how do people pass their time in Toyland?"

"They play and amuse themselves from morning till night. Then they go to bed, and in the morning they begin all over again."

"Ummmm!" said Pinocchio and he nodded his head, as if to say: "That sort of life would suit me fine."

"Now, will you come with me? Yes or no, make up your mind!"

"No, no, no, no, and no! I have promised the Fairy that I will be good and I must keep my promise. It's nearly dark so I must get back home. Good-bye, have a pleasant journey."

"Where are you going in such a hurry?"

"I'm going home, the Fairy wants me home before dark."

"Wait a little longer."

"I shall be late."

"Just two minutes."

"And what if the Fairy should scold me?"

"Let her scold you. When she's finished scolding, she'll stop," said the wretched Shoelace.

"Are you going alone or is someone going with you?"

"Alone? No, there'll be more than a hundred of us!"

"Are you going on foot?"

"No, a stagecoach is coming for us at midnight. Why don't *you* come?"

"It's useless to tempt me. I have promised my kind Fairy that I will be sensible, and I don't intend to break my word."

"Well, good-bye then."

"Good-bye, Shoelace, have a pleasant journey. Enjoy yourself, and think of us sometimes."

As he spoke, Pinocchio made as if to leave; then stopped and turning to his friend, he asked: "Are you quite sure that all the weeks in Toyland are made up of six Saturdays and one Sunday?"

"Positive."

"Are you quite sure that holidays begin on January 1, and only finish on December 31?"

"Positive!"

"What a wonderful country!" said Pinocchio smacking his lips with satisfaction.

Then summoning up every ounce of willpower, he added quickly: "Well, good-bye and have a good trip!"

"Good-bye, Pinocchio, for the last time."

By this time it was very dark. Suddenly, far away, they saw a little light moving, and heard bells jingling and the sound of a tiny horn, very faint and low, like the hum of a bee.

"It's the stagecoach coming to fetch me. Do you want to come too? Yes or no?"

"But is it really true," Pinocchio asked again, "that children in Toyland never have to work?"

"Never, never, never!"

"What a marvellous country! What a really marvellous country!"

CHAPTER THIRTY-ONE
Pinocchio runs away to Toyland

AT LAST THE STAGECOACH arrived. It drove up without a sound for the wheels were wrapped in rags.

It was drawn by twelve pairs of donkeys. They were all the same size, but some were grey, some white, some spotted, and some had broad yellow and blue stripes. But the strangest thing of all was that every one of the twenty-four donkeys, instead of being shod, wore men's white calfskin boots.

The driver was a little man, broader than he was long, soft and oily like butter, with a small face like a red apple, a tiny mouth that was always laughing and a soft caressing voice that sounded like a cat mewing for cream.

All the boys were enchanted by him; and they pushed and shoved to get in first.

As soon as the stagecoach stopped, the little man turned to Shoelace, and with a thousand bows and grimaces, said with the sweetest of smiles: "Tell me, my fine friend, would you like to go to the country where everyone is happy?"

"Yes, I'd love to go."

"But, my dear friend, you can see there's no room; the coach is full."

"Never mind," replied Shoelace, "I can ride on the shafts."

And so he jumped astride the shafts.

"And you, my lovely lad," said the little man, looking admiringly at Pinocchio, "what are you going to do? Are you coming with us, or are you staying behind?"

"I'm staying here," replied Pinocchio. "I'm going back home. I want to work hard and be a credit to those who're bringing me up."

"Come with us, we'll all be so happy," shouted a chorus of a hundred voices.

"If I come with you, what will the Fairy say?"

"Don't worry about her. Just think that we're going to a country where we do nothing from morning till night except enjoy ourselves."

Pinocchio did not reply: he only sighed. He sighed a second time, and a third. At last he said: "Make room for me: I'm coming, too."

"We're full up," replied the little man, "but to show you how pleased I am that you're coming with us, I will give you my seat."

"What will you do?"

"I'll walk."

"No, I can't let you do that. I'd rather ride one of the donkeys!" cried Pinocchio. After several attempts Pinocchio managed to stay on the very temperamental donkey he had chosen, helped by the little man and his cruel handling of the donkey.

Pinocchio was amazed to hear his donkey cry and speak: "The day will come when you'll weep like me but then it'll be too late."

The stagecoach rattled on and at daybreak next day they reached Toyland, safe and sound.

Toyland was like no other country in the world. Its entire population was made up of children. The eldest were fourteen and the youngest barely eight years old. The din and shouting and hullabaloo in the streets were enough to drive one mad.

Children swarmed everywhere. Some were riding bicycles or wooden horses; others were playing blind man's buff or hide-and-seek. Some of them were dressed as clowns, and pretending to be fire-eaters, some were play acting or singing, or turning somersaults. Others were walking on their hands or rolling hoops, or, dressed as generals, were marching along wearing paper hats while others were dressed as toy soldiers.

As for the noise, they were saluting and laughing, and shouting and clapping their hands; some were whistling; some were cackling like hens about to lay eggs. There was such pandemonium and such a wild rumpus, it was deafening, unless you put cotton-wool in your ears. In every open space, there were little theatres which were crowded all day long.

As soon as they set foot inside the city, Shoelace and the other boys who had come with the little man hurried to join these children, and in a few minutes, they were all very good friends, and no one could have been more content and happy than they were.

Time passed like lightning.

"Oh, what a fantastic life!" exclaimed Pinocchio, every time he bumped into Shoelace.

"You see now that I was right," Shoelace remarked. "And to think you didn't want to come! Only a really true friend does favours like that!"

"Yes, you're quite right, Shoelace. Today I'm a perfectly contented boy thanks to you."

Five months passed in this paradise, then Pinocchio woke up one morning, to a most unpleasant surprise.

CHAPTER THIRTY-TWO
Pinocchio grows donkey's ears

PINOCCHIO WOKE UP and began to scratch his head; and while he was doing this he . . .

He noticed that his ears had grown several inches longer!

Now puppets have very, very small ears; so small that they are not visible to the naked eye. So Pinocchio was astounded to discover that overnight his ears had grown so long that they looked like two brooms.

He hurried to find a mirror but he could not find one: so he filled the hand-basin with water and looked into that. There he saw the last thing on earth he wanted to see: a magnificent pair of donkey's ears!

He began to cry and scream and beat his head against the wall, but the more he wept, the longer his ears grew. They even became hairy at the top.

A pretty little squirrel, who lived on the floor above him, heard his shrieks and came down to see what was the matter.

"I'm afraid you have donkey fever!"

"I've never heard of it!" replied the puppet, although he knew only too well what she meant.

"Then I'll tell you about it," replied the Squirrel, "for in two or three hours you'll no longer be a puppet, or a boy . . . You'll be a perfect specimen of a donkey, just like the ones that draw carts and carry vegetables to market."

"Oh! Poor me! Poor me!" cried Pinocchio, seizing his ears with both hands, and twitching and jerking them angrily, as if they belonged to someone else.

"My dear," said the Squirrel to console him, "what will be, will be. It's destiny. The Decrees of Providence state that all those lazy children, who can't abide books and schools, must, sooner or later, turn into donkeys."

"Is that really true?" sobbed the puppet.

"Only too true! It's no good weeping now. You should have thought of that before."

"But I'm not to blame: it's all Shoelace's fault!"

"Why did you follow the advice of such a false friend?"

"Because . . . because, dear little Squirrel, I am a heartless puppet, with no sense at all. If I'd had the tiniest bit of heart, I'd never have left the Fairy. She loved me like a mother and did so much for me! I could be a real boy now! If I meet Shoelace, he'd better look out! I'll fix him . . .!"

He started to leave the room, but in the doorway he remembered his ears, and he was ashamed to be seen. So he put on a large cotton cap and pulled it right down to his nose.

Then he went out to find Shoelace. He looked everywhere, but no one had seen him.

At last he went to his house and knocked on the door.

"Who is it?" asked Shoelace.

"Pinocchio," said the puppet.

"Wait a minute and I'll let you in."

Half an hour later, the door was opened. Shoelace was wearing a large cotton cap that came down right over the end of his nose.

Seeing him like this Pinocchio was consoled a little and said to himself: "Has he got donkey fever, too?"

But he pretended not to notice anything, and said with a smile: "Will you do me a favour, Shoelace?"

"Of course, with all my heart."

"Will you let me see your ears?"

"Why not? But first I want to see yours, dear Pinocchio."

"No, you first."

"No, my dear, you first, and then I'll show you mine."

"Well," said the puppet, "as we're good friends let's make a bargain."

"Let's hear it."

"We'll take off our caps at the same time. All right?"

"All right."

"Now, ready!"

And Pinocchio began to count in a loud voice: "One! Two! Three!"

At "Three!" they took off their caps and threw them in the air.

When Pinocchio and Shoelace saw that they were both in the same boat, they began to wag their long ears and laugh at each other.

They laughed and laughed until their sides ached: but suddenly Shoelace was silent; he staggered and turned pale as he exclaimed: "Help, help, Pinocchio!"

"What's the matter?"

"I can't stand up straight."

"Neither can I," cried Pinocchio, stumbling and groaning.

As they spoke they had to go down on all fours and began to run around the room on their hands and feet. As they ran, their arms turned into legs, their faces grew longer and became muzzles, and their backs were covered with light grey hair, spotted with black.

But the most terrible moment came when they felt their tails sprouting. This was the last straw. They felt so ashamed they began to weep.

But the sound that came out was braying. They brayed in chorus loud and clear: "Hee-haw! Hee-haw!"

There was a knock on the door, and a voice cried: "Open this door! I am the driver of the stagecoach which brought you here. Open up or it will be all the worse for you!"

CHAPTER THIRTY-THREE

Pinocchio is sold to
a ringmaster

THEY DID NOT OPEN the door, so the little man kicked it open and said with his usual chuckle: "Hurray for you! You brayed very well; I recognised you at once. And now here I am."

Hearing these words the two donkeys stood very still, with their heads bowed, and their tails between their legs.

At first the little man stroked and patted them; then he took out a comb and groomed them until they looked a picture. He bridled them and took them to market, hoping to sell them for a good price.

Shoelace was bought by a farmer whose donkey had died the day before: Pinocchio was sold to the ringmaster of a circus.

The coachman was nothing but a cruel little monster, although he seemed all milk and honey. He travelled the world with his coach and his promises and caresses, and rounded up all the children who hated school and books and carried them off to Toyland. When the children turned into donkeys, he took them to market and sold them. In a few years he became a millionaire.

Pinocchio, from the very beginning, led a life of drudgery and was ill-fed and harshly treated.

One morning the ringmaster came into the stable and shouted, "Do you think I bought you just to feed you? You're here to work and help me make money. Come on, do your best! Come into the Circus Ring, and I'll teach you to jump through a hoop and to waltz and polka on your hind legs."

It took three months, with many cuts of the long whip, before the day came when he was ready. His master announced a spectacular show. Brightly-coloured posters were pasted up all round the town.

The performance was a sell-out. You could not buy a seat, not even for its weight in gold. All the ringside seats were filled with boys and girls, who were terribly excited because they were going to see the famous dancing donkey, Pinocchio.

When the Little Donkey Pinocchio appeared in the centre of the ring, the

reaction was stupendous. He was magnificently dressed with a new bridle of shiny leather, with buckles and studs of brass, and a white camellia behind each ear. His mane was divided into tiny curls, each one decorated with a white silk tassel; a broad ribbon of gold and silver ran round his body, and his tail was braided with red and blue velvet ribbons. In short he was irresistible.

The ringmaster made a low bow, and then, turning to Pinocchio, he called out: "Come on, Pinocchio, before beginning your performance, salute this noble audience: the ladies and the gentlemen, and the children!"

Pinocchio obediently bent his forelegs and remained kneeling until the Ringmaster cracked his whip and shouted: "Walk!"

Then the little donkey got up and went round the ring, walking daintily.

After a while the Ringmaster shouted: "Trot!" Pinocchio obeyed.

"Gallop!" – and Pinocchio galloped.

"Run!" – and poor Pinocchio ran like the wind.

Suddenly the Ringmaster raised his arm in the air and fired a pistol.

Pinocchio pretended he was wounded and fell down as if he were dead.

He rose to cheers and applause that could be heard miles away. Naturally, he lifted his head to look at the audience and there in one of the boxes, he saw a lovely lady wearing a large gold chain, from which hung a gold medallion – on it was a portrait of a puppet!

"That's my portrait! That's the Fairy!" said Pinocchio to himself and he was so overjoyed that he tried to cry out: "Oh, dear Fairy! Oh, dear Fairy!"

But instead of these words, all that came out was: "Hee-haw!" so long and loud that the audience laughed, especially all the children.

The Ringmaster, in order to teach him manners, struck him lightly on the nose with the whip handle. The poor donkey put out his tongue and licked his hurt nose, for at least five minutes.

When Pinocchio looked up again, he saw that the Fairy had disappeared! He thought he was going to die; his eyes filled with tears and he began to weep bitterly. However, no one noticed, least of all the Ringmaster, who cracked his whip and cried: "Bravo, Pinocchio! Now show the audience how gracefully you can jump through the hoop."

Pinocchio tried two or three times; but each time he found it so much easier to run under it.

At last he leapt through it but his hind legs caught in the hoop, and he fell heavily to the ground.

When he got up he was lame and could hardly walk back to the stable.

"Pinocchio! Pinocchio! We want the little donkey! Bring on the little donkey!" shouted the children, who were all sorry about his accident. But he didn't appear again that evening.

When the vet saw him next morning, he announced that Pinocchio would be lame for ever.

So the Ringmaster said to the stable boy: "What do I want with a lame donkey? I'd only have to feed him. Take him to market and sell him."

As soon as they arrived at the market a man inquired: "How much do you want for this lame donkey?"

"Five pounds."

"I'll give you five pence, not that he'll be of any use to me. I'm only interested in his skin. He's got a very hard skin and I want to make a drum out of it, for the town band."

You can imagine how Pinocchio felt when he heard that!

As soon as the five pence had been paid, his new master led Pinocchio to a cliff overlooking the sea. He tied a stone round his neck, and a long rope to one leg. Then all of a sudden, he pushed the poor animal over the cliff.

Pinocchio, with that heavy stone around his neck, went straight to the bottom of the sea; his new master held on to the rope and sat down and waited for Pinocchio to drown so that he could skin him.

CHAPTER THIRTY-FOUR
Pinocchio is eaten by the fish.

WHEN PINOCCHIO HAD been under water for nearly an hour, his new master said to himself: "That poor little lame donkey must surely be drowned by now! I'll pull him out and make a wonderful drum out of his skin."

He began to pull on the rope he had tied to one of the donkey's legs: he pulled and pulled, and pulled and pulled and, at last, something appeared on the surface of the water . . . But instead of a dead donkey, there was a live puppet, wriggling like an eel.

When he saw the puppet, the man thought he must be dreaming.

When he had recovered a little, he said, stammering: "Where . . . where's the little donkey I threw into the water?"

"Here, it's me!" replied the puppet, laughing.

"You?"

"Me!"

"Ah, you rascal, don't try and fool me!"

"Fool you? Of course not, my dear master; I am perfectly serious."

"How is it, then, that an hour ago you were a little donkey and now you're a wooden puppet?"

"When I was drowning, the kind Fairy sent an immense shoal of fish to eat me."

"I'm not in the least bit interested in your story!" cried the man in a rage. "I paid five pence for you, and I want my money back! I know what I'll do! I'll take you back to the market and sell you for firewood."

"Sell me if you like; I don't mind," said Pinocchio.

But as he spoke he jumped as far as he could, and landed in the sea with a splash; and as he swam away happily he shouted: "Good-bye, master! When you want a nice dry drum, let me know."

Pinocchio was swimming hard, but with no real idea of where he was going, when he saw a rock that looked like white marble. On that rock, a little goat was bleating and beckoning him. The strangest thing about all this was that the goat's hair was bright blue, a lovely blue that reminded him of that child he had met so long ago.

Pinocchio's heart began to beat faster and faster! He redoubled his efforts to reach the rock. He was more than half-way there when what should he see, rushing towards him on the surface of the water, but a great sea-monster. It had a horrible head and its mouth, which was like a dark cavern, was wide open, showing three rows of razor-like teeth. Even a picture of them would have been frightening. It was a huge shark.

Pinocchio was petrified. He tried to dodge it, and twisted and turned in the water, but that vast cavern of a mouth came right for him, as swift as an arrow.

"Hurry, Pinocchio, for pity's sake!" bleated the little goat.

And Pinocchio shot forward like a bullet from a gun. He was close to the rock and the little goat was leaning out over the sea, holding out her front hoofs to help him out of the water . . .

But it was too late! The monster had reached him and drawing in his breath, he swallowed him, as if he were an egg.

When he came to, he didn't know where he was. All around him there was darkness; so total that it seemed as if he'd dived into an inkwell. He listened but he could hear nothing; only every now and again, a great blast of wind hit him in the face. At first he did not know where it came from, but he soon realised that it was coming from the monster's lungs. The Shark suffered badly from asthma and when he breathed it was like the north wind blowing.

At first Pinocchio tried to pluck up a little courage; but when he was convinced that he was imprisoned inside the Shark, he began to weep, saying: "Help! Help! Will no one save me?"

"Who can save you, you miserable wretch?" said a voice in the darkness. It sounded like an out-of-tune guitar.

"Who's there?" said Pinocchio, turning cold with fear.

"It's me. I'm a poor Tuna fish, I was swallowed up with you. What sort of fish are you?"

"I'm not a fish. I'm a puppet."

"If you aren't a fish, what are you doing here?"

"I didn't come here *willingly*; I was swallowed. What are we going to do?"

"We must wait for the Shark to digest us."

"But I don't want to be digested!" screamed Pinocchio.

"I don't want to be digested, either!" continued the Tuna fish, "but I am enough of a philosopher to realise that for a Tuna, it is better to die under water than drown in oil."

"But I want to escape . . ." insisted Pinocchio.

"Escape, if you can!"

"Is this Shark very big?"

"His body is more than half a mile long, without counting his tail."

While they were talking, Pinocchio thought he saw a gleam of light very far away.

"What do you think that little light is?" asked Pinocchio.

"It's probably one of my companions in distress."

"I'm going to try and find him. It could be an old fish who could tell me how to get out of here."

"I hope so, dear puppet."

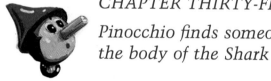

CHAPTER THIRTY-FIVE

Pinocchio finds someone in the body of the Shark

PINOCCHIO BEGAN TO FEEL his way inside the Shark's body, working along, step by step, towards that tiny, flickering light, far far away. As he walked, his feet slipped in puddles of fat and greasy water, and there was such a strong smell of fish, that it very much reminded him of Lent.

He walked and walked and walked, and at last, when he reached the light, what did he find but a little table, all set, with a candle in a green bottle, and sitting at the table was an old man, as pale as if he were made of snow or whipped cream. He was eating live fish, that were so much alive they hopped out of his mouth while he was eating them.

When he saw who it was Pinocchio almost fainted. He wanted to laugh, to cry, to say so many things, instead he managed only a few incoherent words. At last he was able to let out a cry of joy and opening his arms wide,

he threw them around the old man's neck, shouting as he did: "Father! Father! Oh, I've found you at last! I'll never leave you again, never, never, never!"

"So my eyes don't deceive me?" said the old man, rubbing them vigorously. "Are you really my dear Pinocchio?"

"Yes, yes, it's really me! You haven't forgotten me? Oh! dear Father, how good you are! And to think that I . . . Oh! but when you hear what has happened to me, how often things have gone wrong . . ."

So Pinocchio told Geppetto all his adventures and how he had despaired when he saw the boat capsize.

"I recognised you, but how could I get back?" said Geppetto. "The waves were so high, then I capsized. A horrible Shark, near by, swam to me and, sticking out his tongue, gobbled me up as if I were a jam tart."

"How long have you been in here?" asked Pinocchio.

"Two years, dear Pinocchio, that have seemed like two centuries!"

"How have you survived? And where did you find that candle? And the matches to light it?"

"In that same storm, which overturned my boat, a cargo ship was also wrecked. The sailors were all saved. The Shark's appetite was excellent that day, and after he'd swallowed me, he swallowed the ship, too. All in one go, he only spat out the mainmast because it got between his teeth, like a fish bone.

"Luckily for me the ship was laden with preserved meat, biscuits, toast, bottles of wine, raisins, cheese, coffee, sugar, candles and matches. But now there's nothing left in the pantry and this candle is the last one."

"Then, Father," said Pinocchio, "there's no time to lose. We must find a way of escaping, right now!"

"Escaping? How on earth are we going to do that?"

"We can get out through the Shark's mouth, throw ourselves into the sea, and swim for shore."

"That all sounds wonderful, dear Pinocchio, but I can't swim."

"It doesn't matter, I'm a very good swimmer. You can get on my back and I'll take you to dry land."

"It's no good, my boy," replied Geppetto, shaking his head and smiling sadly. "Do you honestly think that a small puppet like you, could possibly swim with me on your back?"

"Let's try! If we are meant to die, at least we'll die together."

Without another word, Pinocchio took the candle, and leading the way, he said to his father: "Follow me, and don't be afraid!"

88

They travelled on for some time, on and on through the body of the Shark. When they came to its great throat, they stopped to look round, and decide the right moment to escape.

The Shark was very old indeed and since it suffered badly from asthma and palpitations of the heart, it always slept with its mouth wide open: so when Pinocchio came to its throat and looked upwards, he could see a broad band of starry sky and a large bright moon.

"We must leave now," he whispered, turning to his father. "The Shark is sleeping like a dormouse, the sea is calm, and it's as light as day. Come on, follow me, and soon we'll be free."

They climbed up the monster's throat, and when they got to the immense mouth, they tiptoed along the tongue, which was as long and broad as a garden path. They were just about to jump into the sea when the Shark sneezed so violently that they fell back into its stomach.

The candle went out, and father and son were left in the dark.

"Now what shall we do?" said Pinocchio anxiously.

"My son, we are well and truly done for!"

"Why? Give me your hand, Father, and be careful not to slip."

"Where are you going?"

"We must try again. Come with me, and don't be afraid."

With these words Pinocchio took his father by the hand and they tip-toed back up to the monster's throat. Before jumping into the water, Pinocchio said to his father: "Now get on my back, and hang on tight. I'll do the rest."

As soon as Geppetto was settled on his back, Pinocchio jumped into the water and began to swim. The sea was calm, and the moon shone brightly, and the Shark slept so soundly that not even a cannon firing would have woken him.

CHAPTER THIRTY-SIX

Pinocchio the puppet becomes Pinocchio, the real live boy

WHILE PINOCCHIO WAS swimming for the shore, with all his might, he noticed that his father was shivering violently, just as if he had a fever.

"Bear up, Father, we'll be safe and sound on dry land very soon."

"Where is the shore?" inquired the old man, becoming more uneasy every moment and squinting like a sailor threading a needle. "All I can see is the sky and the sea."

"I can see dry land," said the puppet. "I'm like a cat, I can see better at night than by day."

Pinocchio tried to appear cheerful but he was beginning to feel discouraged. He was growing weaker by the minute, breathing was harder and the shore was still far away.

He swam on as far as he could then he turned to his father and said in a broken voice: "Father, help me . . . I'm dying!"

Father and son were just about to drown together, when a voice like an out-of-tune guitar spoke: "Who's dying?"

"It's me and my poor father!"

"I recognise that voice! You're Pinocchio!"

"That's right: and who are you?"

"I'm the Tuna fish from the Shark's tummy, don't you remember?"

"Yes, how did you escape?"

"I followed your example."

"Dear Tuna fish, I beg you, for the love of your children, help us, or all is lost!"

"With all my heart! Take hold of my tail, and let me tow you. You'll be on dry land in four minutes."

Geppetto and Pinocchio accepted the invitation without further ado: and decided to sit astride the Tuna.

"Are we too heavy?" asked Pinocchio.

"Heavy! Why it's like having two empty seashells on my back," replied the Tuna fish, who was about as big and strong as a two-year-old calf.

Arriving at the beach, Pinocchio jumped off first, and then helped his father down. He turned to the Tuna fish, and, in a trembling voice, said: "My dear friend, you have saved my father's life! How can I ever thank you? Will you allow me to give you a kiss as a token of my everlasting gratitude?"

The Tuna fish put his nose out of the water and Pinocchio, kneeling on the ground, gave him a great big kiss. At this sign of real affection and gratitude, the Tuna fish, not wishing to be seen crying, dived under the water and was gone in a flash.

Geppetto was so weak he could scarcely stand so Pinocchio took his arm and said: "Lean on me, Father, and let's be on our way. We'll walk as slowly as snails, and when we're tired, we'll stop and rest."

"And where shall we go?" said Geppetto.

"We'll look for shelter, some bread, and a little straw for a bed."

They hadn't gone very far, when they saw two ugly faces, by the roadside, begging from passers-by.

"They were the Fox and the Cat, but how they had changed. The Cat was really blind now; the Fox had grown old, and his fur was so moth-eaten, it had disappeared on one side, and one day he was so desperately poor he had been forced to sell that handsome tail to a pedlar as a fly-swat.

"Oh, Pinocchio," whined the Fox. "Give something to us poor invalids."

"Invalids," repeated the Cat.

"Good-bye, swindlers," replied the puppet. "You fooled me once, but never again."

"Don't abandon us!"

"Us!" repeated the Cat.

"Good-bye! Remember the old saying: 'He who steals his neighbour's cloak, dies without a shirt on his back!'"

Pinocchio led Geppetto peacefully on their way, but they hadn't got very far when they saw, at the end of a path, a pretty little cottage made of straw with a tiled roof.

"Someone must live here," said Pinocchio. "Let's knock."

"Who is it?" said a tiny voice from inside.

"A father and his son without bread or a roof over their heads," replied the puppet.

"Turn the handle and the door will open," said the tiny voice.

Pinocchio turned the handle, and the door flew open. They both went in but could see no one.

"Where's the master?" said Pinocchio in astonishment.

"Here I am, up here."

Father and son looked up, and there on a beam was the Talking Cricket.

"Oh, my dear Cricket!" said Pinocchio, with a polite bow.

"So, I am 'dear Cricket' now am I? Don't you remember when you threw a mallet at me?"

"You're quite right, Cricket; throw a mallet at me, too, but please have pity on my poor father."

"I will have pity on you both; but I thought I would just remind you so that you can learn that we should always treat each other as kindly as possible."

"You're right and I will always remember your lesson. But how did you manage to buy this pretty cottage?"

"It was given to me yesterday by a lovely goat, with beautiful blue hair."

"What became of the goat?"

"I don't know."

"When will she be back?"

"She won't be back. She left yesterday, very sad, and bleating as if to say: 'Poor Pinocchio, now I'll never see him again! The Shark must have eaten him by now!'"

"Did she say that? Then it could only have been the Fairy, my dear Fairy!" shouted Pinocchio, sobbing his heart out.

When he'd had a good cry, he dried his eyes and made up a comfortable bed of straw for Geppetto. Then he turned again to the Cricket and said: "Where can I get a cup of milk for my father?"

"Giangio, the gardener, lives three fields from here, he has cows. If you ask him, he may let you have some."

Pinocchio ran all the way to Giangio's house; but the gardener said: "How much milk do you want?"

"I only want a cupful."

"A cup of milk costs a penny. First pay me the penny."

"I haven't even got a farthing," replied Pinocchio, very sadly, ashamed of himself.

"That's too bad," replied the gardener. "If you have no money, then I have no milk."

"Never mind!" said Pinocchio and turned to leave.

"Wait," said Giangio, "perhaps we can come to some arrangement. Will you turn the windlass for me?"

"What's a windlass?"

"It's the machine that draws up water for the orchard."

"I'll try."

"Well, if you draw up a hundred buckets of water, I'll give you a cup of milk."

"I'll do it."

Pinocchio set to work at once, but before long he was dripping with sweat. He had never worked so hard.

"My donkey used to do this job," said the gardener, "but the poor beast is dying."

"May I go and see him?" asked Pinocchio.

"Of course you may."

When Pinocchio entered the stable, he saw a handsome donkey lying on the straw. He was dying of hunger and hard work. Pinocchio looked closely at him and said, "I think I know this donkey". Bending over him he said in donkey dialect: "Who are you?"

The donkey opened his eyes and stammered: "I . . . am . . . Shoe . . . lace . . ." and then he died.

"Oh, poor Shoelace!" murmured Pinocchio, and taking a handful of straw, he dried his tears.

"Are you feeling sorry for a donkey that cost you nothing?" said the gardener. "What shall *I* do, I paid cash for him?"

"He was . . . my friend."

"Your friend?"

"He was at school with me."

"What!" roared Giangio, bursting out laughing.

The puppet now felt so ashamed that he didn't answer, but took his cup of milk and returned to the cottage.

From that day, for more than five months, he got up before dawn every morning and turned the gardener's windlass in order to earn the cup of milk that was doing his father so much good. And he also learned how to weave baskets from reeds. He sold these and made just enough to live on. He also made a handsome cart so that he could take his father out for some fresh air.

Every evening he practised his reading and writing. For a few pennies he'd bought a large book in the nearby town. He made a pen out of a thin twig and having neither ink nor inkwell, he used a little bottle of cherry and blackberry juice instead.

In fact, by hard work and thrift, his father was able to live quite comfortably. Pinocchio was even able to save two shillings to buy himself a suit.

One morning he said to his father: "I'm off to market, today, to buy myself new clothes. When I return," he added, laughing, "I'll look so smart that you'll think I'm a prince."

He felt very happy indeed as he ran along. Suddenly, he heard someone calling him; he turned and saw a pretty snail crawling out of the hedge.

"Don't you recognise me?" said the snail.

"I'm not sure . . . Perhaps . . ."

"Don't you remember the blue-haired Fairy's maid? Don't you remember when I came downstairs to let you in, and found you with your foot sticking through the door?"

"Of course I do!" cried Pinocchio. "Where is the good Fairy? What is she doing? Has she forgiven me yet? Does she still remember me? Does she still love me? Is she far from here? Can I go to her?" Pinocchio asked all these questions in one breath; but the Snail replied with her usual deliberation: "My dear Pinocchio, the poor Fairy is in the hospital."

"In the hospital!"

"Yes, I'm afraid so. Weighed down by a thousand disasters, she is very, very ill, and she hasn't even the money for a crust of bread."

"Oh, how dreadful! Oh, the poor Fairy! The poor Fairy! If I had a million pounds, I'd run and give them all to her; but I only have two shillings . . . here they are; I was going to buy some new clothes. Take them and give them to the good Fairy with my love."

"But what about your new clothes?"

"I don't care about new clothes! I'd willingly sell these rags, if it would help her. Hurry. If you come back in two days I can give you a little more. Up till now I've worked to keep my father; from now on, I'll work an extra five hours a day and help keep my mother, too. Good-bye, I'll see you in two days' time."

For a change the Snail began to run like a lizard in summer.

When Pinocchio got home his father asked: "Where's your new suit?"

"I couldn't find one that fitted me. I'll buy one another time."

That evening instead of working till ten o'clock, Pinocchio went on until twelve; and instead of making eight baskets, he made sixteen. Then he went to bed and fell fast asleep. He dreamt he saw the Fairy, looking lovely and smiling. She kissed him saying: "Well done, Pinocchio! In return for your generosity, I forgive all the bad things you've done. Children who love and cherish their parents, and help them when they're sick and poor, deserve love and praise, even if they aren't perfect. Go on like this and you'll be happy."

Then the dream ended and Pinocchio woke up full of wonder. He was amazed to find that he was no longer a puppet but a real live boy!

He looked around but instead of the straw walls of the cottage, he saw a pretty little room, simply but beautifully furnished and decorated. He jumped out of bed, and found a new suit, a new cap, and a shiny new pair of boots.

As soon as he was dressed, he put his hands in his pockets, as boys do, and found a little ivory purse on which were written these words: "The Blue-haired Fairy Returns Pinocchio's Two Shillings and Thanks Him for his Generosity."

He opened the purse and inside, instead of two silver shillings, there were twenty gold pieces, fresh from the mint.

Then he went to look in the mirror, but he didn't recognise himself. He saw a good-looking, intelligent boy, with brown hair and blue eyes, and a wide, happy, holiday smile. Pinocchio really didn't know whether he was dreaming or not. "Where's my father?" he cried suddenly.

He went into the next room and there he found old Geppetto, full of life and just as good-natured as ever. He was carving wood again and was working on a lovely design of leaves and flowers and animals.

"Father, please explain what's happened?" asked Pinocchio, hugging and kissing him.

"All this change is thanks to you," replied Geppetto.

"Why me?"

"Because when naughty children become good, then the whole family is happy."

"But where's the wooden Pinocchio?"

"There he is," replied Geppetto, pointing to a large puppet leaning against a chair with his head on one side, his arms dangling down, and his legs all twisted up under him, so that it was a miracle he could stand at all.

Pinocchio turned and looked at him for a little while, and then he said contentedly: "I was so silly when I was a puppet! How glad I am now that I am a real boy!"

96